# The Detective Is Already Dead

La detective está muerta.

5

nigozyu

Illustration by Umibouzu

Scarlet

Fuubi Kase

Reloaded

Stephen Bluefield

My assistant dragged me around today, just like always. I'm the only one who can keep up with his ██ nature... Still, I did make that contract, so I have to protect him.

The problem is that I'm running out of time. I won't be the Ace Detective much longer. I hope my assistant will find companions who can replace me quickly. After all, SPES isn't the only enemy of the world he'll be fighting. There's ██, who should be a ██, like me, and I'm also concerned about ██. ...No, I really must be overthinking that. Still, this world just might hold some huge secret. I'll make my exit with the expectation that the final hope I'm leaving behind will reveal it someday. Neither ██ of the clock tower nor ██, king of the night, can change this fate. Before too long, I'm going to—

"This six-year story is about to reach its climax."

"Let's all end it together."

# The Detective Is Already Dead

# 5

nigozyu

Illustration by Umibouzu

YEN ON

New York

**The Detective Is Already Dead, Vol. 5**

nigozyu

Translation by Taylor Engel
Cover art by Umibouzu

TANTEI HA MO SHINDEIRU, Vol.5
©nigozyu 2021
First published in Japan in 2021 by KADOKAWA CORPORATION, Tokyo.
English translation rights arranged with KADOKAWA CORPORATION, Tokyo,
through TUTTLE-MORI AGENCY, INC., Tokyo.

Yen On
150 West 30th Street, 19th Floor
New York, NY 10001

Visit us at yenpress.com
facebook.com/yenpress
twitter.com/yenpress
yenpress.tumblr.com
instagram.com/yenpress

First Yen On Edition: January 2023
Edited by Yen On Editorial: Shella Wu, Anna Powers
Designed by Yen Press Design: Andy Swist

Yen On is an imprint of Yen Press, LLC.
The Yen On name and logo are trademarks of Yen Press, LLC.

Library of Congress Cataloging-in-Publication Data
Names: nigozyu, author. | Umibouzu, illustrator. | Engel, Taylor, translator.
Title: The detective is already dead / nigozyu ; illustration by Umibouzu ;
    translation by Taylor Engel.
Other titles: Tantei wa Mou, Shindeiru. English
Description: First Yen On edition. | New York, NY : Yen On, 2021.
Identifiers: LCCN 2021012132 | ISBN 9781975325756 (v. 1 ; trade paperback);
    ISBN 9781975325770 (v. 2 ; trade paperback); ISBN 9781975325794
    (v. 3 ; trade paperback); ISBN 9781975348250 (v. 4 ; trade paperback);
    ISBN 9781975360122 (v. 5 ; trade paperback)
Subjects: GSAFD: Mystery fiction.
Classification: LCC PL873.5.I46 T3613 2021 | DDC 895.63/6—dc23
LC record available at https://lccn.loc.gov/2021012132

ISBNs: 978-1-9753-6012-2 (paperback)
       978-1-9753-6013-9 (ebook)

10 9 8 7 6 5 4 3 2 1

LSC-C

Printed in the United States of America

# The DetECtiVe Is AlreadY Dead

## 5

# Contents

# 6 years ago, Nagisa

For us, it was a routine sight.

"—Nana! I brought lots. Which one do you want?"

Afternoon sunlight streamed into the hospital room.

The pink-haired girl who'd called me by my nickname dumped an armful of picture books onto my bed, then started lining them up. She was trying to choose one to read aloud.

"Um, Ali? I'm already twelve. You really don't need to read to me…"

I knew she was doing it to be nice, because I was physically weak and couldn't go outside. I appreciated the thought, of course, but…

"This one, then!"

Yeah, she wasn't listening. She never did.

Instead of her usual diary, which she'd been writing in just a minute ago, she opened a picture book and started reading it, enthusiastically and loudly.

She had an energetic, charming voice.

I got the feeling that just listening to her voice might cure me. …Though being read to was still a bit too childish.

Gazing fondly at Ali, I spoke to the other girl in the room. "What are you reading, Siesta?"

A girl with white hair was sitting in a chair in the corner with a book. For some reason, she had a code name, "Siesta," and she seemed rather mysterious. She had to be about the same age as Ali and me, but she seemed more mature than you'd expect. She had what I guess you'd call a philosophical air about her; I thought it wouldn't hurt for her to be a little more childlike and honest…even though I was a kid myself.

"It's the tale of a prince who was both happy and unhappy," Siesta said. I assumed that was a description of the story rather than its title.

A prince who was unhappy but happy... What did that mean?

"What's it about?"

Ali had stopped reading the picture book and joined our conversation. Absolutely everything interested her, but she also got bored with things twice as fast as the average person. In a good way, we could probably stand to learn from her free-spirited behavior.

"It's about a statue of a kind-hearted prince who shares his treasures with the poor people of his city." Siesta closed the book gently, then closed her eyes just as softly.

"What a nice guy!" Ali sat down in a chair near me and started swinging her feet back and forth.

So it was a story about a compassionate, wealthy prince helping his citizens? ...So where did the "unhappy" bit come from?

"The thing is..." Siesta opened her eyes, and they were rather sad as she told us the rest of it. "The treasures he gave them were pieces of himself."

"What do you mean?" Ali asked. "He didn't have a lot of money and watches and things?"

"No. The kind statue was covered in gold leaf and decorated with jewels. He gives his own body away to the poor, bit by bit."

"...He loses parts of himself?"

The thought of that prince's devotion, his literal self-sacrifice, gave me an indescribable feeling. My chest grew tight.

"A ruby sword. Sapphire eyes. The gold leaf that covered his body. When the statue of the prince had given all these things away to the townspeople, he looked very shabby. All he had left was his heart, which was made of lead."

As she said that, Siesta gently placed her hand on the left side of her chest.

"That poor statue!" Ali cried out. Even if it was just a story, she felt genuinely sorry for that prince.

Trying to save somebody, even if it meant sacrificing yourself—it was a noble act, but it also seemed terribly sad.

*  *  *

"But that's not where this story ends."

I raised my head, as if Siesta's voice had pulled me out of sleep.
"This statue had someone precious who understood him."
""He did?"" Ali and I asked in unison.
"That's why the title of this book is what it is, too."
Then Siesta began to tell us about the lone swallow who remained with the statue.

The tale of a small black bird who stayed by the side of the one he loved to the very end, even though no one could see why.

# Chapter 1

## ◆ One year later, the adventure resumes

"Have you calmed down a little?" Siesta asked outside the bathroom.

"......Yeah."

In the bathtub, I gave a small sigh of relief.

While lecturing me about how I couldn't have a healthy mind in an unhealthy body, Siesta had half forced me into the bath. She was right; my physical and mental strain had eased, and my brain fog was slowly clearing.

"Shave your stubble while you're at it."

"Yeah."

"Can you wash your back by yourself?"

"Yeah."

"And don't pee in the tub."

"...What am I, a kid?" I smiled wryly. How old did she think I was anyway?

"Well, I don't know how much you've grown." Siesta sat down; I could see her back through the frosted-glass door. "'Give a guy three days to grow, and you might not recognize him at the end.'... Remember? You're the one who said it," she told me.

I'd forgotten until she mentioned it. "Yeah, I guess that's true." In our case, it had been way more than three days.

Today, Siesta and I had truly reunited for the first time in a year.

"I never dreamed you'd still be living in this apartment, though."

Siesta's light laugh drifted to me from the changing room.

She'd used the master key, one of her Seven Tools, and walked into my place like she owned it. Just like before.

"...The 'I never dreamed' bit is my line."

At dawn on the day I'd fought Ms. Fuubi, I'd sworn I'd get Siesta back someday.

Of course, I'd known it wasn't going to be easy. That was why I'd been prepared to put everything I had on the line. But right now, that wish had really—

"You're...not SIESTA, right?"

A memory of the maid flickered through my mind, and I asked without really thinking. After all, you couldn't tell the two of them apart just by their appearances.

"Are you stupid, Kimi?" That old familiar line zinged back at me from the changing room. "We've talked for this long and you still aren't sure?"

"...Yeah, good point."

*Only one person in the world scolds me that way—and it's you, Siesta.*

That meant I'd gotten my wish.

Even so, I couldn't be 100 percent delighted about it. I'd lost something irreplaceable in exchange.

"But it sounds as though she did make contact with you."

Just when my eyes were threatening to go misty again, Siesta's voice broke in. From the gist of the conversation so far, I assumed she was talking about SIESTA the maid.

"Yeah. I got through that problem you assigned me."

Through the maid, Siesta had given each of us a task to handle and had shown us the way to resolve our worries and problems. Her one miscalculation had been that the future we'd chosen was different from the ending she'd imagined.

"Where is she now?" I asked the original Siesta. When I'd run into SIESTA at the former SPES facility a few days ago, she'd been living inside a computer terminal, but...

"Carrying out a different task. She's the one who gave me the master key before I came here."

Come to think of it, I'd returned the key to her at the lab. Did that mean she'd guessed Siesta would wake up all along?

"Siesta..." *How in the world did you wake up?* I was about to ask the question, but I swallowed it back down.

I didn't have to ask. I knew.

Siesta was probably aware as well. That was why she was here.

"What I need to do now is rescue our friends. That's one more reason to defeat Seed as soon as possible." That had to have been Siesta's dearest wish for four years—for six. Before she met me, she'd encountered Seed on that island. He'd defeated her and stolen all her memories of the facility, his organization, and her companions. Even so, she hadn't forgotten her mission; she pursued Seed, and had spent three whole years fighting SPES with me.

At the end of that story, Siesta had lost her life. However, she'd managed to transfer her heart and mind into the body of her enemy Hel—aka Natsunagi. After that, Siesta and Hel had consolidated their memories, and Siesta had reclaimed the ones she'd lost.

"I'd forgotten some important things," Siesta said quietly on the other side of the thin door. "The fact that I met Nagisa six years ago. The fact that I lost Alicia. That past was the last thing I could afford to lose, and still..." Her voice was subdued.

Still, I knew better than anyone that Siesta wouldn't back down.

"I won't forget any more. I won't let them steal anything else from me. I won't hesitate. I won't lose. So, Kimi..." Siesta's intense voice seemed to pierce through the door and echo in the bathroom. "I want you to be my assistant, just one more time."

I could see a familiar silhouette on the other side of the frosted-glass door. We'd had a similar conversation here four years ago. I'd turned her down that time. I splashed hot water over my cheeks, then gave my answer. "—Yeah. Make me your assistant again."

It was about time I got out of this tepid water.

"So please, Siesta. Help me find a way to save Saikawa."

A few days earlier, Seed had taken Saikawa to use as a potential vessel for the primordial seed. However, if he was planning to use her that way, he wouldn't kill her.

"Yes. Seed has always wanted a perfect vessel. Hel and I were his top candidates, though. If he's going to use Yui Saikawa instead, it's probably going to require some prep work. I'm sure we still have a chance to save her."

"! So then—"

"It's all right. We'll save Yui too, of course," Siesta declared firmly. But…

"Saikawa 'too'?"

Something about the way she'd said it seemed odd to me. It was as if she thought there was somebody besides Saikawa who needed saving… Was she talking about Charlie? But Charlie was in the ICU, and as frustrating as it was, there wasn't anything we could do for her.

"You can't mean…"

My heart was pounding loudly. I shook my head; it couldn't be that. If it was, though… If something like that was really possible… It was a ray of hope, and I wanted to grab it in spite of myself. After a seemingly endless silence, Siesta said—

"I'm not giving up on Nagisa Natsunagi."

## ◆ Cold memories

"Siesta, what's this about?"

Soon after, I'd gotten out of the bath, then found Siesta in the living room. I wanted to know what she'd meant by not giving up on Natsunagi.

But all she said was, "If you don't dry your hair, you're going to catch a cold." She patted a nearby floor cushion, motioning for me to sit down. "Here, give me your towel."

I sat cross-legged on the cushion, and Siesta got behind me and rumpled my hair with the towel, drying it off. When I looked at the low table, there was a pizza delivery box on top. Siesta must have made the order while I was in the bath.

"You can't have sound thoughts with an unsound body, after all."

So now that I'd washed up, we were going to eat? Remembering I hadn't eaten a thing for the past three days, I opened the box. "...Were pizzas always shaped like Pac-Man?"

"I couldn't quite wait until you were out of the bath." When I took a closer look at Siesta, I saw a piece of cheese stuck to the corner of her mouth.

She hadn't changed. I gave a wry little smile, and then we sat across the table from each other and started on the pizza. It was the first time in a year that we'd had a meal together.

"...This's great," I said.

The comfort food was especially delicious to my tired body. I'd had pizza with Siesta at my place four years ago, too. After that, I'd left on an adventure with her, and we'd spent three dazzling, extraordinary years together.

Whenever we'd gotten through one of our many fights with pseudohumans or survived unforeseen incidents, we'd toasted with Coke and stuffed ourselves silly.

...*This is everything I wanted*, I thought. Taking a bath, eating and talking with somebody who was important to me. But those were privileges exclusive to those of us who were alive. As for those who weren't... Natsunagi—

"Assistant."

The next thing I knew, Siesta was gently drying my eyes with her fingertips.

Had I always been this weak?

"...Sorry."

"This is nothing new."

Siesta and I both smiled wryly at each other.

"I know everything about you, Kimi, weaknesses included. It's fine," she said. She was acting like she was my new parent.

"You don't know about this past year, though."

"True. But..."

At that, Siesta's smile grew troubled.

"I do know you were trying to bring me back to life."

*   *   *

Oh, right. At dawn, just after I'd fought Ms. Fuubi, about ten days ago, I'd declared an oath to SIESTA and to Natsunagi's heart. It must have reached her.

"You're not going to say it?" I asked.

"Say what?"

"The usual."

She could easily call me stupid for it. I thought she should, really. Considering what that wish had ended up doing—

"I won't say it," Siesta told me. I couldn't look her in the face. "I shouldn't."

That made me raise my head. Siesta was looking straight at me. Maybe it was my imagination, but her eyes seemed just a little wet.

"...I didn't think I had the right to say this now." Saying nothing would be the same as lying, though, so I told Siesta the words I'd been keeping in. "I'm glad I got to see you again."

"So am I."

Siesta accepted the thought with a smile, without teasing me the way she used to. Neither of us could be thrilled with the situation in the truest sense of the word, though. Yes, I'd gotten my wish, but this wasn't the ending I'd wanted. I really couldn't call this outcome a "happy" one.

So I asked her one more time: "Hey, Siesta. What do you mean, you're not giving up on Natsunagi?"

"I can't say anything for certain yet, but has anybody actually seen her body?"

Was that what this was? So Siesta didn't know about that yet... The momentary glimmer of hope was snuffed out.

"—I did. I held her hand and felt it growing colder."

What I'd seen three days ago came to mind. Something sour worked its way up from the pit of my stomach.

On that day, lying in a hospital bed, I'd heard about Natsunagi's death from Ms. Fuubi. I hadn't wanted to believe it. Setting my feelings aside, believing it seemed wrong somehow.

After all, a year ago, I'd made a big mistake regarding Siesta's death. At the time, I'd lost some of my memories to Betelgeuse's pollen; Ms. Fuubi had told me about her death later on, but what I'd heard hadn't been the truth.

Because of that, I'd decided I couldn't take Ms. Fuubi's statement at face value and had bolted out of my hospital room. ...Then I'd run into a doctor. The man had said he was the director of the hospital and shown me to a certain room. And there...

"Natsunagi was lying on a bed, unconscious, hooked up to a ventilator." There were all sorts of tubes connected to her body. It was like every available scientific technology was trying to preserve this one girl's life.

"Then Nagisa really is still..."

"Alive? That's what I thought, too."

True, there was no way to know how the situation would progress, but Natsunagi wasn't dead. There had to be a possibility of saving her. ...Or so I'd hoped, until the doctor kept talking.

"*Nagisa Natsunagi is brain-dead.*"

The term meant exactly what you'd expect. The brain had lost all function, and the possibility of recovery was zero. The patient would never wake up again. In most countries around the world, a person was considered officially dead when their brain died.

Thanks to the ventilator and medication, her EKG was still undulating quietly, but even that wouldn't last long. As Natsunagi didn't have any relatives, there was no one to make the decision to take her off the ventilator, so she'd simply been kept on.

Her condition had changed suddenly, and they'd closed her room to visitors. Just before, I'd held her hand for the last time. It had been as cold as ice, which wasn't right for a girl with such a summery name.

"I see..." After she'd heard the story, Siesta lowered her eyes in thought. "So we can't confirm Nagisa's current condition."

Exactly. As I'd said a minute ago, no one was allowed to visit her at this point. In fact, if you thought about it in terms of what turning away visitors meant, I could guess what had happened to her. Natsunagi really was—

"We don't know what her condition is." As I responded to Siesta, I erased the conclusion my mind had already drawn. "I do know someone who might know how she ended up like this, though."

"You mean..." Siesta seemed to have thought of the same person. Her eyebrows furrowed.

"That's right. Your junior—Mia Whitlock."

### ◆ The maid dances in the dead of night

"I see. So you met Mia, too."

Siesta and I were in the back seat of a car, on our way to a certain *destination*.

Mia Whitlock was the Oracle, one of the twelve Tuners who protected the world. She had the ability to foresee major turning points in history. About a week ago, in search of a way to bring Siesta back to life, Natsunagi and I had flown to London to see her.

"Yeah, we talked about you a lot."

I remembered the conversation I'd had with Mia, who was apparently Siesta's junior, that day. How SPES had come to possess the sacred text and the resolution Siesta had made behind the scenes—

"Are you angry?" Siesta asked without looking at me. "I hid so much from you during those three years."

...She really had. She'd hidden the true nature of the enemy we were fighting, for example. She'd called herself the Ace Detective but hadn't explained what it meant. Her friendships, too. She'd never told me any of the important stuff.

"If there was a reason you needed to keep it a secret, then I could never be mad. But..." I could feel Siesta turn to look at me. "Sacrificing yourself— that's the one thing I can't let go."

I wanted to tell that to both detectives, not just this one.

"...You're right," Siesta said quietly, and returned to gazing out the window at the setting sun. "Still, who'd have thought Mia would be in Japan?" Shifting gears, she smiled. "I haven't seen her in a year."

Last time a future she'd predicted had changed, Mia had visited Japan to confirm it in person. This time, the Ace Detective had come back to life, and the world had reached a major turning point; there was no way the Oracle wouldn't come to observe it.

"And you think Mia may be able to explain Natsunagi's current state?"

"Yeah. At the very least, she should know what's happening that I don't know."

That was why we were on our way to talk to her. About a week ago, on top of that clock tower in London, Mia and Natsunagi had a secret conversation. We were in a car bound for *a certain location* where we might find Mia and learn what they'd discussed.

"But, Siesta, are you okay?"

Siesta cocked her head as if she didn't know what I meant.

"I mean, you did just wake up, and we're already on the move…"

I'd realized quite late I'd brought Siesta out here without giving any thought to her physical health.

"I haven't deteriorated so badly that I need you worrying about me, Kimi," she murmured with her eyes closed. Apparently I'd been worried for nothing. "Besides, there isn't much time."

"True." It couldn't be much longer before Seed made Saikawa his vessel. "Can we go a little faster, Siesta?" I asked our driver.

The girl sitting behind the wheel shot me a glance in the rearview mirror. "I don't appreciate being ordered around by you, Kimihiko."

It was the former maid-type Siesta; she'd come back with the original Ace Detective. Her body had been returned to Siesta, though, which meant this one was brand new…

"What's the matter? Have you been captivated by the new me?" Siesta asked with a straight face, registering my gaze.

"I mean, you can tell yourself that, but you don't look any different."

The girl was still identical to Siesta. The only differences were the maid uniform and the fact that she wasn't wearing a hair clip.

"Yes, because this is 'me.'"

Up until a little while ago, a mysterious doctor, based in SPES's laboratory, had been repairing Siesta. Did that mean he was the one who'd made this body?

"Unfortunately, my current design isn't meant for combat. However, now that both my body and heart are mechanical, I wouldn't have minded being a fighting maid robot," SIESTA went on. As she spoke, her expression in the rearview mirror didn't change.

"The 'mechanical heart' bit doesn't make sense to me," I told her. "All else aside, there's no way anyone who can make a wish for somebody else is just a machine."

She'd wanted to save her mistress, even if it meant going against orders. If her heart was capable of a contradiction like that, then it was definitely the real thing.

"Right, Siesta?"

"...Yes. I never thought you two would surprise me so much." Coming from her, that was a frank admission of total defeat, but she seemed to be smiling as she said that. "We'll have to think of a name for you, then."

Siesta's eyes focused on the driver's seat. True, SIESTA should probably have a new name, both to celebrate her new life and to make it easier to tell the two of them apart.

"You'll name me?"

Stopping the car at a red light, SIESTA blinked at us in the rearview mirror.

Siesta leaned forward from the back seat and slipped a moon-shaped hairpin into SIESTA's pale silver hair. "Your name is Noches," she told her.

For a girl who'd been weighed down with a daytime moniker up until now, that did seem like an apt new name.

## ◆ The truth of that day, the last wish

"It's been a week, huh, Mia?"

The person we'd hoped to find was there when we reached our destination, and I heaved a sigh of relief.

"You really have no manners, do you? Telling me you want to see me out of nowhere like that..." Sweeping her pale blue hair back with one hand, Mia Whitlock glanced at me. She was wearing the shrine maiden outfit she always wore when performing her duties. "I believe we'd agreed that I would contact you if there were any developments."

Along with the matter of Natsunagi, I'd asked Mia for a certain favor. I wanted her to keep an eye out for the world's next crisis...for Seed's appearance. I knew it wouldn't be that easy, but I'd turned to her anyway, trusting that it would help me find Saikawa.

"Sorry. The situation's changed a bit."

With a few meters between us, I faced Mia. Behind her, Japan's capital city spread out as far as the eye could see. This was the observation deck of the nation's tallest radio tower; just like her clock tower in London, Mia Whitlock had been conducting her duties in a place where she could look out over the city.

"...It's just you?" As Mia spoke, she gazed out the windows at the urban landscape bathed in the warm glow of the setting sun.

She and I were the only ones here, and there wasn't a single person in the gallery, either... In other words: "If you're looking for Siesta, she's not here now."

When I said that, her shoulders flinched a little. I knew even without asking that had been her biggest reason for coming to Japan.

"We got *dragged into* a little incident on our way here. Siesta's getting it sorted out."

"So, nothing's changed there." With a small sigh, Mia turned back to me. "And? *Why are you actually here?*" Her straightforward lilac eyes bored into me. From this point on, lies and evasions wouldn't be tolerated. That was just how I wanted it, though.

"Well, there was something I wanted to check on."

I took a few steady breaths then asked my question:

"Natsunagi's heart is what brought Siesta back to life, right?"

Siesta and I had come to that conclusion without even talking about it. One year ago, when Siesta had lost her heart and her life, her body had been put in cold storage and preserved in suspended animation. That meant just one piece was needed in order to truly bring her back to life: her heart.

Siesta had used the power of her "seed" to transfer her own consciousness to her heart. So if it were to be returned to her body… If her body and spirit were linked again, then Siesta would come back to life. The idea itself was simple enough.

However, there was one major issue: The all-important heart was in Natsunagi's body. When Natsunagi had fought with Siesta as Hel, her heart had sustained damage, and she'd attacked people indiscriminately in London, trying to find a replacement for it. The heart she'd finally found had been Siesta's. If Natsunagi were to lose it again, she'd—

"That's right." Mia looked at me. There was no change in her expression. "Nagisa Natsunagi picked up on that possibility. She asked me, if she died and the heart *were returned to its owner*, whether the Ace Detective would come back to life."

Then I'd guessed right. Back then, Natsunagi had already braced herself. She'd thought that her death might revive Siesta.

That was why she'd made that promise to me last week in London: "I'll get Siesta back, no matter what I have to do."

No matter what she had to do. Even if that meant sacrificing herself.

"And you didn't stop her, Mia?" I squeezed my fists until I felt my nails dig into my palms.

"No."

"—Why not…?!"

"Well, I mean—!" Mia's protest echoed in the observation deck. "That's what happens when you change the future!"

Her shoulders were quaking. She was angrier than she'd ever been, and she was crying harder than I'd ever seen her. With tears rolling down her cheeks, she raged at me, or maybe at herself. "No matter how hard the choice is, if there's a wish we really and truly want, we—"

…Oh, I see. That was what I'd asked Mia to do. I'd asked her to help me revive Siesta, to help me find a new route that would make it possible. And these were the consequences.

A year ago, Siesta had died, and her heart had kept Natsunagi alive.
Now Natsunagi was dead, and her heart had brought Siesta back to life.
Route X had been the only one that could bring about the miracle I'd
wanted, and this was how it ended.

"I guess I made you do it."

That was true for both Mia and Natsunagi. There was no way I could
blame either of them.

"No matter what you sacrifice, no matter what price you pay, keep working to get that wish of yours." Those had been Bat's last words to me.

I'd thought I'd braced for the worst long ago, but what I'd resolved to do
was swallow that seed. To offer myself, basically. Even if the seed took part
of my body or a few years of my life, if it made it possible to revive Siesta,
I would've been glad to make the sacrifice.

...But I hadn't realized Natsunagi probably thought the same way. I
hadn't noticed just how badly she wanted Siesta back, nor did I pick up on
her passion.

Natsunagi had met Siesta six years ago, long before I had. Then Seed had
stolen both their memories, they'd encountered each other as enemies, and
finally, they had parted in death.

However, that separation had been a result of Siesta's devotion to Natsunagi. Natsunagi had wanted to relive her life, to experience going to
school, and Siesta had used her own heart to make that wish come true.
When Natsunagi retrieved her memories of the incident, she'd resolved
to save Siesta even if it meant sacrificing herself. There was nothing unnat-
ural about it.

"Nagisa smiled. She seemed relieved," Mia told me, wiping her tears
away again and again. "She wasn't originally intending to die, of course.
Even so, she said she'd finally be able to do the job she needed to do as a
detective. That she'd be able to repay her debt to both you and Siesta."

"......!"

That wasn't right. Natsunagi wasn't the one who hadn't repaid her debt.
It was me.

"I asked Nagisa if she wasn't afraid, if she was really all right with this.

And she said..." Mia gazed out the window, into the distance. "She said she was only returning what she'd borrowed. That this was the correct route."

"That can't be. Why the hell would I want that future?"

"Yes. I didn't think it was correct, either. How could I?" With her eyes on the sunset, Mia spoke quietly. "That choice couldn't be the right one. At the very least, I knew that it wouldn't be the future you wanted, Kimihiko Kimizuka. You'd tried so hard to persuade me, and and you did. I wanted to help you... And if this was the result, after all that, I wouldn't blame you if you wanted to hit me. And yet," she went on, "I couldn't deny Nagisa's choice. Her passion."

A single tear rolled down Mia's cheek.

Had she cried like this a year and a half ago, when she'd failed to stop Siesta's gamble?

"I don't know how to face Boss. I betrayed her wish and prioritized Nagisa's. And so—"

"—That's wrong."

Just then, a voice that didn't belong to either of us echoed throughout the observation deck. Mia turned around. Her gaze focused on a spot right beside me.

"It's been a long time, Mia."

The two heroes, the Oracle and the Ace Detective, reunited for the first time in a year.

## ◆ The Ace Detective swears a second oath

"Boss..."

Mia Whitlock stared at the white-haired ace detective, stunned.

She'd known that Siesta had come back to life, or at least that the possibility existed. However, she'd only understood it in a logical, factual way.

This reunion really should have been impossible, and Mia stood frozen, tears streaming down her face.

"You're still a crybaby, I see." Beside me, Siesta was smiling.

"...I don't recall crying that often in front of you, Boss." Mia looked away apologetically.

Siesta watched her. Then, for some reason, she sighed and glared at me. "Kimi, I do think you should stop trying to make girls cry. It's a bad habit."

"Who'd do that on purpose? No one wants to see that."

"Granted, the fact that you haven't changed is a bit of a relief..."

"That's a terrible thing to be relieved about." Although, since that predisposition of mine hadn't changed either, I had to admit I'd caused her trouble just a minute ago.

"Besides, it's my cue at times like these."

Siesta took a step toward Mia.

"......!"

Mia's face twisted. She believed she didn't have the right to see Siesta now. "I rejected the future you wanted to protect, Boss. The new route I found took another life. I knew nobody would be happy that way, and I still..."

Mia didn't think this outcome was the right one, either. Back then, though, she'd had no choice. She hadn't been able to ignore Natsunagi's feelings and had gotten the opportunity to clear her regrets over having been unable to save her benefactor...but another detective had paid the price.

One week ago in London, Mia had taken a step forward. However, she hadn't necessarily been heading toward the future she'd hoped for.

"I'm sorry." Mia spoke from the heart. Her eyes were red, and her head was facing down. "Once again, I failed to stop the Ace Detective's gamble. I knew it might be a mistake, but I couldn't do a thing. I'm... I'm..."

"That's not it." Interrupting Mia, Siesta pulled her into a hug. I could see Mia's startled face within Siesta's arms. "First of all, I'm the one who needs to apologize. I'm sorry, Mia."

"Boss, why should you...?" Mia didn't seem to understand what Siesta was trying to get at. Her round, lilac-colored eyes wavered.

"I made you go along with my selfish request, and you got hurt. I want to give you a proper apology for that."

A year and a half ago, Siesta had come up with a plan to make the

enemy steal the sacred text, one that incorporated the possibility that she'd be sacrificed. In order to put that plan into action, she'd enlisted Mia's help.

"...You were only trying to complete your mission as a Tuner, Boss. I just wasn't prepared," Mia murmured. She was crying in Siesta's arms. "And this time, again, I..."

"As I said, you've got that wrong, too." Siesta held both her shoulders, speaking firmly. "This isn't over yet."

Mia's eyes widened.

"It's true that Nagisa's sacrifice brought me back to life. However, *who decided this was where we'd end?*"

Mia and I trembled at her words. Just as I'd sworn not to let the story end until I'd brought Siesta back to life, even in this desperate situation, Siesta wasn't giving up on Natsunagi.

"Listen to me, Mia." On that observation deck, in the heart of Japan, Siesta issued a declaration. "I swear I'll save Nagisa Natsunagi. After all, she didn't give up on me."

Siesta was swearing that oath to the two of us, and maybe to herself.

"...Really?" The Oracle's voice sounded very childlike.

As she dried Mia's tears, Siesta smiled.

"Yes. I prefer stories with happy endings."

## ◆ The order rings out

"I'm sorry."

A little while after that, Mia bowed her head to us again.

It wasn't a continuation of that earlier conversation, though.

"No matter what I do, I can't see the future that's affected by the primordial seed."

I'd wanted Mia to take a look at the future that revolved around Seed, but it hadn't worked. "That can't be helped. I know you can't just see what you want to see."

"That's true as well, but..." Mia kept darting glances at me, as if she had something else she wanted to say.

"What? Is it hard to talk about?"

Not that any of the people around me are shy.

"I think she's trying to say it's your fault, Kimi."

...The first and finest example being the white-haired girl next to me.

"You're saying I'm the reason Mia can't see the future? That's crazy talk." But when I looked at Mia, she averted her eyes uncomfortably. ...*Wait, seriously?* "What did I do?"

"You changed the future," Siesta said briefly. "In the one I had in mind, you and Nagisa, Charlie and Yui would have defeated SPES. Or Seed, rather. Granted, that was only what I hoped would happen, but even so."

That had been Siesta's last wish, and Natsunagi, Charlie, Saikawa, and I were the legacy she'd left behind.

"But from there, you started down a path even I hadn't envisioned."

...Yeah, that's right. I hadn't been able to give up on her, and I'd started searching for options with Natsunagi and the others. Neither the Oracle nor the great detective had seen that coming.

That had landed us where we were now: Natsunagi was dead, Saikawa had been taken captive by the enemy, and Charlie was in critical condition. This route couldn't have been further from what Siesta had hoped for, or from my own ideal.

"The future is incredibly unstable right now." Mia had been listening to us with her eyes closed; as she spoke, she opened them again slowly. "Because of your actions, there is no set route regarding the battle with Seed any longer. There's nothing I can observe now, including who will win or how it will happen."

That was the conclusion Mia Whitlock the Oracle had come to. Even the Tuner who saw the future couldn't see how this story would end.—But...

"Our loss isn't set in stone, either." True, this was nothing like how I'd visualized it would be. I'd lost three precious friends. But our last hope was still standing next to me. "Isn't that right, Siesta?"

I gazed at that "hope," the Ace Detective.

If the future was undecided, then we'd defeat the world's enemy with our own hands and rescue all our friends. That was the ending Siesta was aiming for.

"Yes. That's why I came back."

Siesta's fleeting smile wasn't confident, like one a hero of a story would have worn. Right now, though, when we couldn't see the light, just having her with me made me believe I could still make it until tomorrow.

"Assistant." Siesta pointed at my chest, and I realized my phone was vibrating in my jacket's inner pocket. I checked the name on the display, then picked up.

"Hey, you damn brat. Finally got out of bed, huh?"

I heard someone blow cigarette smoke on the other end of the line.

It was Fuubi Kase, the person who'd first told me Nagisa Natsunagi was dead.

"Ms. Fuubi. It's like I thought—we can't give up on Natsunagi…"

"Kimihiko Kimizuka," an ice-cold voice said from the receiver. "If you've got time to cling to hope, then pick up your weapon."

…Yeah. That was the sort of person Fuubi Kase was.

She'd been assigned the role of Assassin, an ally of justice—no, an enemy of evil—who eradicated the world's crises. She didn't cling to temporary emotions or 1 percent chance of hope. She believed in nothing but solid logic and the strength she herself had built up, and she used those things to defeat the enemies of the world. It wasn't long before I realized a situation where we'd need them was bearing down on us.

"_____!"

The crisis began with a sudden ringing in my ears.

It felt as if an enormous bell was clanging right next to me. My head throbbed, and I felt sick to my stomach. The phone fell from my hand, and I dropped to my knees.

"Kimihiko? …Boss!" Mia ran to me, but her eyes promptly turned to Siesta. Apparently Siesta and I were the only ones this mystery phenomenon was affecting.

"What's…this…?" Like me, Siesta was kneeling on the floor. She grimaced, holding her chest.

"The enemy's attacking," Ms. Fuubi said from my dropped smartphone. Just then, I heard a distant explosion.

"What now...?" The headache and nausea had finally receded a little, so I got to my feet and looked outside. "What's...happening?"

From above, at a height of four hundred and fifty meters, I saw enormous tentacles attacking a cluster of skyscrapers.

## ◆ Plant City 20XX

"What the heck is this?"

Once Siesta and I had recovered from the mysterious bouts of nausea, we'd left the radio tower and raced to the scene. However, the sight before us was so bizarre that I stopped in my tracks.

The sun was down. Long, thick roots, which looked like enormous tentacles, were coiling around the cluster of skyscrapers. An astronomical number of vines had wrapped around an elevated railway line, trapping a train. The streets were in complete pandemonium. People panicking ran this way and that, accidents were breaking out everywhere—smoke permeating as flames shot up.

"Assistant!"

Just then, a powerful shock ran through me.

"...?!"

The next thing I knew, I was lying on the asphalt, and Siesta was covering me.

A moment later, a pedestrian signal crashed down right beside us. The weird plants were tangled around its support pole. I should have given a little more thought to why there were so many traffic accidents.

"What's going on?"

Taking Siesta's hand and getting to my feet, I looked around again. The ground had split, and roots choked the buildings. Traffic signals and signs had been destroyed, and many people had already abandoned their cars. This city was in the process of being conquered by plants... Or, actually, by the primordial seed.

"Assistant, look." Siesta pointed urgently. A tentacle had attacked a young man who hadn't evacuated fast enough. It coiled around and around him, then carried him off.

"Siesta, we're going after it!"

What was the enemy planning to do with kidnapped civilians this late in the game? Seed's main objective wasn't to attack the human race...

"We'll never make it in time if we just chase it." Pulling me by the hand, Siesta dashed up the fire escape of a nearby building. From that high vantage point, she watched to see where the tentacle went.

"That's..."

A distant commercial-use building that was taller than the rest had been punctured throughout by an enormous tree. In the crown of that tree, I could see what appeared to be a *big, ripe, swollen fruit.*

"Yui Saikawa is there." Siesta was peering through a pair of binoculars. She pointed at the upper floors of the building. "She and several civilians are trapped inside that giant fruit."

"Is she okay?!"

"She looks limp. She may be unconscious."

—Still, now we knew where we had to go.

"Those trapped civilians are probably serving as *nourishment.* Nutrients are being drained away from them and used to cultivate Saikawa, the vessel."

I see. Cultivating the vessel...or maybe repairing it.

During the fight a few days earlier, Saikawa had sustained injuries even Seed hadn't seen coming. He was probably trying to heal her damaged body, to restore her strength as a vessel. At this point, the process was most likely in its final phase.

"Siesta, let's hurry." We'd learned the enemy's objective and where our friend was. In that case, we didn't have time to hang out on these stairs and watch. "We need to get to Saikawa fast—"

Before the words were out of my mouth, *my body rose into the air.*

"Assistant!" Siesta screamed; she was peering down at me. It wasn't until then that I realized I was falling. In the same moment, a vine had stretched up from the ground and destroyed the stairway.

"____!"

Even if I managed to land using proper form, I was plunging toward concrete from ten meters high. Was landing safely even possible? Hoping that the seed I'd swallowed had made my body a bit sturdier, I kept falling—

"Hm?"

A few seconds later, I collided with something, but the impact was nowhere near what I'd expected. When I dubiously opened my eyes, I saw...

"Hey, you damn brat. Now you're indebted to me for life."

The irritating redheaded policewoman was cradling me in her arms, looking triumphant.

"...How many kilograms of force do you think that was? Hundreds?" Staring at Ms. Fuubi's face at close range, I forced a smile. I weighed a shade under sixty kilos. Not only that, but when you considered how far I'd fallen straight down...

"Don't underestimate the police. I can carry an African elephant in one hand."

...That's really scary. I don't think I'll be defying her again, ever.

"Assistant!"

Siesta made a clean landing on the asphalt. She might be a little late, but she'd just casually pulled off a superhuman feat of her own.

"It's been a while, Ace Detective." Ms. Fuubi grinned. She didn't seem startled to see her. It was as if she'd already known Siesta had come back to life.

"I do feel bad for having caused trouble for you after my death." Siesta gave an apology that only someone who'd been resurrected could give. "I'm also grateful that you protected the others, Charlie included." But even as she spoke to Ms. Fuubi, her eyes were cold.

"Hm? Oh, yeah, I'll give him back." Joking around, Ms. Fuubi lowered me to the ground.

"And? What's the situation?" Siesta asked. Since Ms. Fuubi had called us about this, she had to know something.

"From what I hear, it all came out of nowhere. A huge tree grew up through a building that was smack in the middle of town; then the ground fissured and plants started attacking people. Right now, even the police are panicking." Ms. Fuubi sighed.

"And Seed is nearby, too?" I asked. If our enemy had triggered a situation this massive, I couldn't imagine that he wasn't here.

"Good question. I dunno what he looks like."

"I don't suppose you're Seed, are you?" Siesta inquired casually. Come to think of it, about a year ago in London, Seed had made contact with us disguised as Ms. Fuubi.

"Ha! *Did your deductive skills dull while you were dead?*" Ms. Fuubi dismissed Siesta's question with a laugh. "If I were the enemy, I would have killed that brat a second ago."

Oh, yeah, probably. So this was the genuine Fuubi Kase, then.

"In that case, are you sure you're okay with this?" Siesta watched Ms. Fuubi dubiously. "The mission of defeating SPES was assigned to me, the Ace Detective. You're the Assassin; ordinarily, you wouldn't be allowed to help me with this."

That was a rule set by something called the Federal Charter. Since there were countless global crises, they were each handled by a predetermined Tuner. Seed's attack had been assigned to the Ace Detective.

"Help you? Nah. I was just cleaning up after you people." Ms. Fuubi gave us a mean little smile. "For now, I'm taking a temporary break from my Assassin work. I'll evacuate the civilians; you focus on rescuing Yui Saikawa and defeating the enemy."

Then she tossed her survival knife to me. "I'm off to do my duty as a police officer," she told me, red ponytail swaying. Her expression was bursting with confidence.

"Let's go, Assistant," Siesta said, and the two of us started toward Saikawa again. We were headed for the retail building we'd seen from the stairs, the one that had fused with the huge tree. Pushing upstream against the fleeing crowd, we raced to the scene.

"How are we going to rescue Saikawa?"

"I suppose we'll just have to climb up the side of the building—Wait, remind me: Can you do things like that?"

"I'm surprised you thought there was even a one percent chance that I could."

"Hmm. Maybe I should have stolen that spider-fellow's ability," Siesta said. She was talking about a pseudohuman we'd defeated ages back.

Come to think of it, did Siesta know I'd swallowed Chameleon's seed? The seed was a double-edged sword; it gave you special abilities, but in exchange, you had to sacrifice one of your senses or some years of your life. If Siesta knew I'd eaten it so I could get her back, what would she say? Would she be worried for me, or—?

"Assistant?"

My silence seemed to strike Siesta as odd. She turned back, staring at me.

"No, it's nothing. Let's hurry," I said, making a run for my friend.

"Yes. Seriously, do hurry. I've been matching your pace all this time."

"...I'm starting to think it would be faster if you carried me piggyback."

## ◆ That was how we did things

From the scramble intersection, we looked up at the eight-story shopping mall. A huge tree grew straight up through its center, and thick branches had broken through windows and walls.

"Saikawa..."

In the crown of the tree, which was practically part of the structure now, we could see a fruit-like object. Saikawa and other regular citizens were trapped inside its eye-catching ripe skin.

"It doesn't look like scaling the outside is going to work."

"Then we'll just have to go through the inside, huh?"

That enormous tree had suddenly sprouted and impaled the building. There was no telling what the inside would look like. Even if we made it up to the fruit, we wouldn't be able to rescue everybody at once. If we could retrieve Saikawa, though, the flow of nutrients should stop, and that would save the civilians.

As I was thinking, I looked up at the building again and spotted a heli-copter in the dark sky. Were they taking an aerial survey of the damage?

"...Hm?"

Just then, a long, thin tentacle stretched up out of nowhere and grabbed *the helicopter's tail rotor.* There was only one way I could see that playing out.

"Assistant!"

Even before I could move, Siesta's sharp voice hit me, followed by the rest of her: She'd tackled me, pushing me to the ground to protect me. The next instant, an explosion pierced my ears.

"......! Siesta!"

We were a good distance from the crash, but even then, an intense blast of heat hit us. The black smoke was so thick, I couldn't open my eyes. I called out to the detective...but there was no answer. I couldn't even sense her presence. *No way...* I raised my head, and just then, a gunshot rang out. The bullet split the wind, cutting through the smoke.

"It's a hundred years too early for you to worry about me."

Siesta stood in front of me, musket at the ready. She knew I'd never catch up to her.

Beyond the distant flames from the explosion, I spotted the silhouette of an enemy I'd seen just the other day.

"—It's been a long time, but I see you haven't changed." Out of the grad-ually clearing smoke, Seed spoke to Siesta. He normally couldn't tell humans apart, but Siesta had been a candidate vessel, so perhaps she was a special case.

"You, on the other hand, take on a different shape every time I see you." Siesta was expressionless. She must have been watching her enemy trans-form ever since their first encounter six years ago.

However, Seed looked nearly the same as he had when I'd met him a week ago. His long white hair was mixed with strands of gray, and he wore armor that came up to his neck. His face seemed lifeless, his features androgynous. He had the eyes of a creature that had abandoned all emo-tions and everything else. As if he'd cut them off and thrown them away.

"I do think you used to be a bit more human, though," Siesta said unexpectedly. Even if Seed was a plant that had flown here from outer space, Siesta seemed to imply that he'd once resembled us.

"What are you getting at?" Granted, Seed didn't seem able to understand human words. He cocked his head, mystified.

He wasn't playing dumb. He also wasn't doing what Hel did when she'd been pretending not to notice her feelings of love. The fact that Natsunagi had bombarded him with her strong emotions and still hadn't managed to defeat him was proof: The primordial seed had nothing resembling feelings.

"Enough arguing. I've already issued *the order*." Four tentacles stretched from Seed's back, and thick briars grew from the cracked ground. The seeds he'd sown all over the world were ready to sprout.

"The vessel will be complete soon. For now, I'll eliminate the enemies who threaten my survival instinct."

Then Seed's tentacles and the tips of all the plants under his control streaked toward us. As he said, there would be no resolving this through debate. We were heading into the genuine final showdown.

Still, even if he'd taken damage the other day, would we have a fair fighting chance against him? It was nighttime, so we couldn't expect any help from the sunlight that made him weak.

"What do we do, Siesta?" I asked, coming up to stand beside the world's most reliable partner.

"It's fine. I've got an idea."

Yeah, that's it. This reassuring feeling. She'd always protected me this way, with that big metaphorical umbrella of hers. Yes, she'd picked me up just like this, and...

"...Hm?"

Throwing me over her shoulder, Siesta started forward and skillfully dodged tentacles as they stabbed into the ground. Then, leaping as if she were taking flight, Siesta *threw me past Seed*.

"Not fair!"

I tumbled right into the entryway of a building. The exact one we were here for, so—

"Take care of Yui."

"...For once, could you explain what you're doing before you do it?"

## ◆ To all living creatures

Looking back, whenever Siesta said she had a good idea, it was usually a bad one for me. I didn't have time to complain right now, though.

"I'll be back in ten minutes."

Turning away from the battlefield, I set off to rescue Saikawa.

Ten minutes. Would Siesta be able to withstand the enemy's attacks that long? For now, I had to believe in her. She'd chosen to send me, and I needed to respect her choice. Besides...at this point, I couldn't see her choosing to sacrifice herself.

I made my way through the mall, the former heart of a space for teenagers. Just a few hours ago, it must have been bustling with people, but now it was changed beyond recognition.

"So I can't use the escalators or the elevators."

The building's power was out, and it was dark. The huge tree stretched up through the center of the floors, and viny plants grew thickly all over the place. Pushing my way through them, I spotted a stairway.

I was pretty sure this building had eight floors. From there, I'd have to get up to the roof, then jump down onto that big fruit. I had a mental image of how it should go, but would it really be that easy to rescue Saikawa? ...There was so much to think about that it was giving me a headache.

Siesta was fighting with Seed, and Saikawa had been captured. Charlie was still in the hospital in critical condition, and Natsunagi—

".........!"

As a rule, nothing I did could change their fates, and I knew there was no point in thinking about it now. Even so, as I ran up the stairs two at a time, the girls' faces came to mind.

I'd been alone. The next thing I knew, though, they were with me, by my side. I'd gained so many things that were important to me, without even meaning to. When people found something more precious than themselves, I was sure they—

"!"

I saw a figure huddled on the landing between the fourth and fifth floors.

"Are you okay?"

Was it a shopper who hadn't gotten away in time, or a civilian who'd been snatched by a tentacle? I couldn't see that well in the dark, but I reached out toward the hunched back.

"—Gah, aaaaaaaaah!"

The huddled figure gave a piercing shriek, then whipped around and leaped at me.

Like a zombie, it made a grab for me. It wasn't as strong as I'd thought, though. I swept its feet out from under it, pinned it, and held a gun to its head.

"You're…"

My gun was trained on an enemy I'd met on the battlefield many times: Chameleon.

"…No."

It didn't take me long to realize this wasn't the actual Chameleon I'd fought. *It was a doll.* When I'd encountered Seed at the SPES laboratory a year ago, he'd been cutting off bits of his own body and making temporary clones. This doll was probably something similar; it didn't have as much strength as a pseudohuman, and it was hard to define it as either animal or plant.

"Forgive me."

Even so, I murmured to it briefly, then shot through its head. The Chameleon doll shriveled up; it was like watching a plant die in fast-forward.

"—I, w—"

At last, with a strangled whimper, the doll vanished.

*Ow?*

I thought about what that expression of pain meant.

Was the impulse to scream from pain different from "emotion"? Seed had no emotions whatsoever. In that case, the clones he'd created—

"Complete the mission," said a voice behind me.

When I turned, there were enormous, razor-sharp claws right in my face.

"—!" I lost my balance but managed to dodge, then got a good look at my attacker. "You're as huge as ever, Cerberus."

The pseudohuman Cerberus was a hulking, priestlike man who was around two meters tall. Just as he'd done during our previous encounter, he had transformed fully into a beast-man.

"Sorry, but I don't have time to deal with you, either." With no hesitation, I pulled the trigger, finishing the enemy with three shots.

"—I, wa—" Cerberus cried in a thin voice. This was another hastily made plant doll. It would have taken a lot more than that to stop the real Cerberus, but with those three shots, he toppled toward me, apparently dead.

He was two meters tall, and yet, as his body fell against me, he seemed to weigh practically nothing. He began to dry up and crumble away. At the very end, the proud wolf murmured something in my ear.

"—I want to live."

*I want to live.*

Not *Ow.* They'd been saying they wanted to live.

Both Chameleon and Cerberus. All living creatures. They all want to survive, to live. Just as I'd wanted to bring Siesta back from the dead and had wanted Natsunagi to live.

"Everybody's like that."

Belatedly, I understood. The fear of death was a basic emotion, an instinct nobody could deny. Dolls, plants, pseudohumans... When I let those words affect me, I almost forgot.

Hel and Bat, of course, but also Chameleon and Cerberus, and the clones I'd fought all this time—They feared death just as ordinary humans did. They got angry and occasionally showed other emotions.

The *loyalty* Cerberus felt toward Seed, the *sadism* Chameleon inflicted on Natsunagi, and the *hostility* he'd showed me. Those were all clear examples of feelings. That's right: Unlike the primordial seed, the clones had unmistakable emotio—

"—No, that's wrong."

Like a jolt of electricity, one theory raced through my brain. Maybe I'd— maybe *we'd*—had the wrong idea all this time.

"That's why you..."

Just then, a tremor made me stumble. There was a fierce battle going on outside, and I had no time to stand still. I hurried for the roof.

## ◆ Until we take them all home someday

I raced up the stairs and finally reached the door at the top. I shot out the lock, then kicked the door down and stepped outside.

"—! Here too?"

The crown of the great tree had burst out onto the roof, covering the whole space with thick branches and leaves. Pushing my way through them, I made for the edge.

"Saikawa!"

When I looked down, I saw the enormous fruit clinging to the wall of the building a few meters below. From a distance, it had looked like a distorted semicircle, but from this angle, it was closer to a cross-section of a pomegranate. Saikawa and the other sleeping figures were surrounded by globules of dark red pulp.

Steeling myself, I jumped down onto the fruit—and luckily, it was sturdy enough to hold the weight of another human, because I managed to land safely.

"If I cut these stems..."

Thick plant stems were tangled around Saikawa and the bodies of several civilians; they seemed to be transporting nutrients, as if they were pipes. Pulling out the survival knife Ms. Fuubi had loaned me, I began to cut through them one by one. However, it was a process of trial and error—

"Give me a break already!"

A tentacle that had penetrated through the wall of the building reached toward me. It seemed to have grown out of the great tree that pierced the mall, and I guessed this was a defense system, meant to drive away *undesirables*.

"—!"

There was a total of three tentacles now. Hastily leveling my gun, I fired one shot, two…and realized I was out of bullets. I had no way to avoid the third tentacle. *Not good*, I thought—but then I noticed I had an incoming call.

"—You saved my butt, Charlotte."

A third bullet sliced through the wind and blew the last tentacle away.

"As expected of you. You've got to be five hundred meters from here."

Guessing where she was from the angle of the shot, I spoke to her through my wireless earphone, keeping my eyes fixed on the distant building.

"That was nothing," she responded after a few seconds. "A first-class sniper can kill an enemy from two kilometers away."

She was tough on herself, as you'd expect from an agent who was training under the world's toughest boss.

"Charlie, are you okay? Ms. Fuubi didn't say a thing…"

It had been three days since I'd first heard that Charlie was in a coma, and Ms. Fuubi was supposed to call me if her condition changed.

"Do you think that woman would take care of me for three whole days?"

…That was disturbingly convincing.

"I'm not okay just yet, so this is the best I can do." She was laughing at herself. She still couldn't move as well as she wanted to.

"That was plenty helpful. But how did you get from the hospital to that building?"

"She brought me here."

Charlie was referring to Noches, who must have told her about Natsunagi and Siesta, too.

"I see. Okay, Charlie, you head somewhere safe as well."

"Kimizuka." Just as I was about to hang up, she said my name. "Take care of our companion."

It was a pretty common line. For anyone who worked as part of a unit or team, it would have been a totally natural exchange. However, coming from Charlotte Arisaka Anderson, the words probably carried several times more weight than usual.

"Yeah, I know." So, as I ended the call, I made sure my short reply had years' worth of feelings in it, too.

"Saikawa, it's time to wake up."

I cut the last stalk, the one that connected Saikawa to the fruit itself, and shook her awake.

"...Kimi...zuka...?"

Saikawa's eyes opened a bit. She wasn't wearing her eye patch, and I caught a glimpse of that distinct ocean blue.

"Yep, I'm one of the Kimizukas. Kimihiko, to be exact." I scooped Saikawa into my arms, princess-style.

"You came...to rescue me?"

"While getting rescued myself, yeah."

Ms. Fuubi and Siesta had both saved me from deep trouble. So had Charlie, just before. I still wasn't strong enough to protect everything that was important to me all on my own. Even now, I'd just happened to score the chance to play hero.

"...You haven't changed at all, Kimizuka." Saikawa gave a wry, mildly chagrined smile. "It's all right. You don't always need to have a punchline ready."

"You're saying it's okay to play the dashing hero every once in a while?" It had been a few days since the last time we bantered. We'd have to finish up this routine after we got down, though... After everything was over. Holding Saikawa, I prepared to jump.

"Yes, but you don't have to act." Saikawa clung to me, and... "You've been dashing as long as I've known you, Kimizuka." She murmured something in a tiny voice, but the wind carried it away.

### ◆ The primordial wish

"Siesta!"

When I returned to the battlefield, I found Siesta a little ways from the building. She had shallow cuts on her forehead and shoulders, but she was steady on her feet.

"That didn't take as long as I expected. I'd assumed you wouldn't be back for another two hours." ...As always, her opinion of me was way too low. I was maybe two minutes late. "And? What about Yui?"

"She's safe. ...We sort of fought at the end, though."

Ultimately, I'd abandoned the idea of gallantly jumping off the building, choosing to play it safe and climb back in through a window instead. Apparently her judgment of me had taken a steep dive. So unfair.

"Ms. Fuubi's taking care of her now, so she's in good hands."

On my way down with Saikawa on my back, I'd run into the redheaded policewoman, who'd attached an anchor-like tool onto the building's exterior wall. She'd asked me to rescue the other people who were trapped in the fruit, and she was currently making arrangements to evacuate Saikawa and the rest.

"So, Siesta. What's the situation here?" I took another look around. Most of the buildings were half-demolished and covered in vines, and the cracks in the ground had gotten worse. This place had lost all function as a city.

"I'd say we're headed into Round Two." Suddenly, Siesta sent a sharp look at one of the destroyed buildings. Soon, from the clouds of dust, someone appeared—

"Seed..."

Seed was swaying on his feet, and part of his armor had crumbled away. The Ace Detective and the enemy of the world must have been equally matched for those ten minutes.

"We rescued Saikawa," I told Seed, coming up to stand beside Siesta. "We'll never let you touch her again. There are no pseudohumans to help you out now. Seed, your plans end here."

I pointed my Magnum at the enemy. In the same moment, Siesta aimed her musket straight at him.

"—Yes, I know. And so I retrieved that seed a short while ago."

For a fraction of a second, I thought I saw a blue flare in the depths of Seed's colorless eyes. ...He couldn't mean he'd used the fruit of the huge tree to extract the seed from Saikawa, could he?

"The vessel this body originally wanted is here."

Eight tentacles stretched from Seed's back, all reaching for Siesta. There were too many of them to repel with bullets, and on top of that, they regenerated fast. We hid in the shadow of a demolished building, riding out the enemy's attack.

"So that's how it is." Wiping sweat and blood from her forehead, Siesta added to Seed's remark. "He's taking another shot at what he tried last year. My heart is inside me now, and my body is undamaged. Seed's trying to secure me as a vessel."

"I see…"

One year ago, Siesta had died and lost her right to become Seed's vessel. However, now that *she'd come back to life*, she was qualified again.

"You don't have to worry, though. I won't become a vessel." Siesta spoke firmly, and her expression was dauntless. "While you were gone, Kimi, I realized something."

"You did, huh? What a coincidence. So did I."

We looked at each other, then exchanged nods. I didn't know if we were both assuming the same thing, but we couldn't be too far off.

"Assistant."

Siesta pushed my head down just as one of the enemy's tentacles pulverized the exterior wall of our building. Using the clouds of dust as cover, Siesta sprinted toward the enemy.

"—I'd predicted that attack already."

Seed's eight tentacles writhed like snakes, trying to catch Siesta in the billowing dust, but she *leapt from one to the next, racing through the air* and closing in on the enemy.

"Siesta!"

Just as she reached the spot directly above Seed, the tentacles formed the shape of an open-mouthed carnivorous plant and attempted to devour this *foreign invader*. Surrounded by a solid wall of feelers, Siesta said—

"I'm too strong for you now."

She shot her way out, scattering fragments of tentacle in all directions. Plunging straight down into the enemy, Siesta blasted a bullet into Seed's neck.

"———!"

Maybe even Seed could feel pain: His face twisted slightly. The neck armor Siesta had fired at fell apart, exposing the skin underneath. In addition to the gunshot wound on the enemy's neck, there was a gash as if he'd been slashed with a large blade.

"You're losing your ability to regenerate," Siesta said. She bounced back, light-footed in spite of the broken ground. "I heard you took a dose of full sunlight and sustained a mortal injury during your fight with Bat. It damaged your cells' capacity for regeneration. Moreover," she continued, revealing another conjecture she'd thought of during this battle, "*in the process of sharing abilities with your companions, you've been weakening yourself.*"

It wasn't clear whether Seed was listening to her or not. His neck was oozing a thick, viscous fluid, and he staggered.

"So although he was creating clones, he wasn't simply replicating," I said.

Siesta nodded. "That's right. Seed makes clones by distributing his seeds with them. That means the more clones he makes, the more power he loses."

Seed had simply been *transferring his power.* As he shared his abilities with his subordinates and scattered seeds across the world, he'd been growing weaker. Siesta had noticed because she'd fought him several years ago, and then again here and now.

Even so, he should have been far stronger than the average pseudohuman, but that's where Bat's desperate gambit had come in: After getting hit with sunlight, Seed's body was having trouble regenerating. Now that the Ace Detective had resurrected, she could fight him as an equal.

"—I don't understand," Seed said. He bent his back forward, his face turned toward the ground. "Why must my power be taken from me and given to my clones?"

He wasn't trying to pull one over on us, and he wasn't playing dumb. He genuinely didn't understand.

"Because that's what you wanted, right?"

I'd reminded him of the wish he'd forgotten.

"Seed, your wish. That survival instinct—"

Then I gave him the hypothesis I'd formed inside that building.

"Its real purpose was to help your descendants survive, wasn't it?"

Seed's tentacle flew at me.

"......!"

Siesta stepped forward and blocked it, swinging her musket at it like a sword.

I couldn't see any anger on Seed's face. That attack had seemed more of a defensive reaction, though, suggesting I'd hit the nail on the head.

"You mean to say this survival instinct doesn't exist for my sake? That I have it merely so that *those things* will live?" Seed asked, temporarily breaking off his attack.

He was talking about Cerberus and Chameleon. He was asking himself whether creating those clones and leaving them on this planet had always been his ultimate wish.

"And that's why I unintentionally shared my power with them? You're saying I did so with the knowledge that it would age me? Such self-sacrifice could never—"

"What's so strange about that? I mean..." I answered Seed's question for him. "You're their parent, right?" At that, Seed's unfocused eyes widened. "That's why you shared your strength *and your emotions* with your children."

All this time, we'd had the wrong idea. It was true that Seed had no emotions now, but that didn't necessarily mean he'd always been like that. Seed had made an emergency landing on Earth fifty years ago and had subsequently infiltrated human bodies, studying their structure. Since he'd learned how to disguise himself as a human, it wouldn't have been odd if he'd acquired human emotions as well.

As a matter of fact, I'd seen signs of it. A year ago, when I'd encountered Seed at SPES's hideout on that deserted island, he'd flown into a rage at Chameleon for interrupting his conversation. It had been a small thing, but it was proof that Seed did feel anger. Besides...

"Chameleon and Cerberus were born from you, Seed. If they had emotions, it's obviously due to their parent's influence."

Essentially, we'd been looking at it the wrong way. Pseudohumans didn't acquire feelings or personalities as they grew. They inherited them from Seed, their parent.

Now that I thought about it, Seed's tone and expressions really were flatter than they had been a year ago. Every time he'd given power to his children, he'd been cutting away his emotions. He'd sacrificed those parts of himself for just one reason.

"You didn't want to ensure your survival. You only wanted to leave your seeds behind."

For living creatures, that was a natural instinct. It was a primitive, inexorable emotion they developed: the desire to leave descendants superseded their desire to survive. However, Seed hadn't noticed that... Or rather, he'd forgotten. A year ago, at that laboratory, Seed had declared that he was going to bury this planet in his seeds, and he'd called it "our objective."

As he made more clones, he'd continued to lose his power and his feelings, and finally he'd even lost sight of his original goal. His bleached-out hair, those eyes that held no hint of emotion—before he'd even noticed, Seed had lost his humanity.

"That's why, Seed," I continued. "You don't want self-preservation. You only want your children, your seeds, to survive on this planet."

That was the final deduction Siesta and I had reached for the story of SPES.

"I see," Seed said quietly. He was standing far away from us. "So that is my ambition. The goal I'd forgotten. My reason for living. The meaning of sowing seeds. My survival instinct—I see, so that's it. I understand everything."

Now, when it was too late, he understood. If Seed had enough emotion left to be self-deprecating, he would probably have spat out the words with a sad smile.

He'd just proved our hypothesis. For the first time, humans and the primordial seed shared a common awareness. We'd reached a mutual understanding. Even so, I quickly learned that this temporary stillness didn't signal the end of the battle.

"If this body's mission is to leave descendants, then I must not die here."

Sprouting one thick tentacle from his back, *Seed stabbed it into his own abdomen.* He immediately gave a brief howl but stood firm.

"Rise again, my comrade."

The fluid that spilled from Seed's stomach spread over a wide patch of cracked ground, soaking in. And then...

"—Gugyaaaaaaaaaaaaaaaaaaaaaaaaaaaaaaaaaaaaaah!"

As if the gates of hell were rumbling open, disaster emerged from the depths of the earth. At first, the stuff seeping out appeared to be liquid, but it gradually assumed the shape of an enormous four-legged beast.

A huge black body: the biological weapon Betelgeuse.

The creature had nothing resembling eyes, but as it gave a loud roar, it definitely *looked* at us. My feet froze in place, but not because I was scared of this monster. Memories of a year ago were flooding my brain, and I couldn't stop them. On that island, this monster had taken Siesta and—

"Assistant!"

The voice that pulled me back to the present was real, not part of that distant memory.

"......! Sorry."

I looked up at the monster again. It was even bigger than it had been last time, and its body was covered with black scales I hadn't seen before.

"—Gaaaaaaaaaaaaaaaaaaaaaaaaaaaaaaaaah!"

The beast had to be at least ten meters long. It mowed down a frozen traffic light, crushed an abandoned car underfoot, and charged straight at us.

"......!"

It really wasn't the sort of opponent we could ward off with guns. Siesta and I sprinted out of its way; unable to stop, Betelgeuse plowed into the building behind us. However, it promptly turned back and zeroed in on us again, as if it had picked up the scent of blood. If this kept up, it would wear us down.

"Assistant."

Just then, Siesta pointed up.

I heard the sound of engines coming from the sky. Reinforcements. Had Ms. Fuubi arranged for them, or was it the official military? A swarm of combat drones appeared from the far side of the moon, preparing to launch missiles.

"That's really nice of them, but..."

"They'll take us out, too."

Siesta and I exchanged nods, then booked it out of there.

Within moments, we heard explosions rain down behind us and felt the heat of the flames. I smelled something burning. Then...

"Gugyaaaaaaaaaaaaaaaaaaaaaaaaaaaaah!"

The roar was so loud that it would have ruptured our eardrums if we hadn't plugged our ears. However, it was proof that the missiles had struck the monster. We dove into a mountain of rubble, shielding ourselves from the hot wind, and watched the thick smoke clear, but...

"Aaaaaaaaaaaaaaaaaaaaaaaaaaaaaah!"

In moments, the monster was howling again. Maybe those black scales prevented any attacks from going through. Ignoring the vortex of flames, Betelgeuse shot out *dozens of tentacles* from all over its body, striking at the unmanned aircraft.

"If any of those crash over here, we'll be in trouble..."

Betelgeuse's tentacles pursued the fleeing drones through the night sky, smacking one then another into the distance.

"Now's my chance." Beside me, Siesta moved. "If I can just get this bullet to penetrate it..."

A red bullet. It was the weapon Siesta had used against Bat four years ago. If that were to hit its target, Betelgeuse's tentacles wouldn't be able to attack her anymore.

While those tentacles were battling the last remaining drone, she ran toward the enemy again.

"—Siesta!"

Just then, though, I felt Betelgeuse's nonexistent eyes turn our way. Its tentacles automatically homed in... The beast's attention had been focused on us all along.

"......!"

Deciding not to run away, Siesta shot the red bullet at the enormous enemy. However, the monster's scales repelled it.

"Siesta!"

My feet were moving before I could think.

Or rather, by the time I yelled her name, I was already right next to her.

"......!"

I covered Siesta, but there was no way I'd be able to shield her from the attack completely. I was ready to die when—

*Skash.*

It sounded like a big blade slashing something apart. I didn't feel any pain, though. That meant it hadn't been the monster's claws gouging my back. In that case—

"Don't you think you should be my partner after all?"

A girl in a black overcoat swept a glowing red saber to the side.

Her long hair streamed in the wind. Through it, I caught glimpses of her profile. It was the face of a girl I would have risked anything to see again.

"Yeah, that wouldn't be so bad—Hel."

## ◆ The three warriors

With a yelp of pain, Betelgeuse retreated. There was a large wound in its right front leg; Hel's red saber had shattered its scales.

"This sword was specifically designed to destroy cells replicated by the primordial seed."

On that battlefield of scorched earth, the girl turned back, lowering the tip of her saber. Her long hair was glossy black, and her crimson eyes blazed. She wore a military-style black-and-red coat, just as she had when I'd encountered her a year ago.

"Come to think of it, you used that sword on Cerberus before..."

I remembered something that had happened the night I first met Hel. Back then, she'd beheaded the pseudohuman Cerberus with one stroke of her sword.

"Yes, and on my own heart," Hel said, laughing at herself. On the day when Siesta had used her brainwashing ability against the black-haired girl, Hel had lost her heart to her own blade.

"Originally, *Father* gave it to me to prevent a rebellion among our kind." Hel looked past the giant monster to where Seed stood limply, a hole in his abdomen, unconscious on his feet. Her eyes narrowed sadly. "I never thought I'd end up using it against him."

The armor over Seed's neck was broken, and there was the large unhealed cut. Who on earth had done that to him, and when…? At this point, I didn't even need to ask.

A few days earlier, in an abandoned building, one girl had risked her life to fight Seed while I was unconscious. This girl in the military uniform was more than just a reinforcement—she was a ray of hope.

"You didn't die, huh, Natsunagi?"

My voice was trembling. Actually, it wasn't just my voice; my legs were shaking so badly that I wasn't sure I'd be able to stay on my feet, and I dropped to one knee.

Nagisa Natsunagi was alive. She'd survived.

"Don't be relieved just yet." The girl in the military uniform sheathed her sword and came closer. "I'm only myself, not Nagisa Natsunagi."

Narrowing her red eyes, she stated the facts calmly. Natsunagi hadn't come back from the dead.

"Besides. It's fine to think of my master, but right now, I wish you'd look at me." Kneeling, Hel placed a finger under my chin, gazing into my eyes from a few centimeters away.

"—Hel," the white-haired detective said. She'd been watching the exchange from nearby.

"Hello there. It's been a long time, Detective." Hel rose to her feet, and she and Siesta glared at each other.

A year ago, these two had fought each other in mortal combat, and now here they were, face-to-face.

"Hel, why are you here?" Siesta asked about her motive for helping us— No, that wasn't all. She was asking what miracle had let her survive.

"I received *Father's order* as well. I believe you two know what I'm talking about."

"......! That ringing in the ears?"

I remembered the noise I'd heard on the radio tower, like the sound of an echoing bell. Why hadn't Mia felt anything weird? Why had Siesta and I been the only ones who heard the ringing? It must have been because we both had a seed inside us.

"My master sustained a lethal wound, so her body temporarily went *dormant*. Father's seed reacted in self-defense."

"Dormant plants... I see..."

Information I'd read somewhere before swirled around inside my head. Such states were a defense system used by plants and other living creatures to keep energy consumption as low as possible while sustaining the bare minimum of biological activity. For example, just as bears and moles hibernate for the winter, living creatures will try to get through abrupt, life-threatening changes to their environments by going to sleep for a while.

That system must have taken root in Natsunagi as well, since she had Seed's survival instinct in the form of his seed. When he lethally injured her, she'd probably unconsciously stopped most of her physical functions, including her brain stem, in an attempt to preserve her life by lowering her energy consumption to the absolute minimum.

"Come to think of it, Siesta also..."

A year ago, Siesta had stopped her own pulse and put herself in suspended animation to ride out Chameleon's attack. Had she been using the same system in her own way?

"When it received that order from Father, the seed in this body began to wake up again," Hel told us, placing a hand on her chest.

The primordial seed's *order* had resonated with every seed he'd sown across the planet. Hel had been no exception: The seed inside her had set her body in motion again, urging her to the battlefield.

—Except...

"But right now, your heart is..." Siesta gazed at the left side of Hel's chest; her expression was full of pain.

She was right. Even if she'd managed to hold on to a faint trace of life by going dormant, and even if the seed had astonishing powers of recovery, right now, Hel's heart wasn't—

"Before I answer that, we'll need to do something about this." Hel's eyes were on the monster. That grave wound had threatened its survival instinct, and it was trembling with rage. Betelgeuse gave a low growl, drooling, and fixed its invisible eyes on the three of us.

"If you want that red bullet to sink in, you'll need to destroy those scales first. ...So? What do you want to do, Miss Ace Detective?" Hel asked Siesta.

"I really don't think I'll ever be friends with you." Without even glancing at her, Siesta heaved a sigh. "Please, Hel. I want you to open a path for me," she said, turning to a previous enemy for help.

For a moment, Hel's eyes widened in surprise—but just for a moment. "I knew it. Having you ask me for favors is quite gratifying." The corners of her mouth rose in a satisfied smile.

"...Don't get the wrong idea. I have no intention of getting along with you."

These two hadn't reconciled, and they certainly weren't companions.

*The enemy of my enemy is my friend*— The white- and black-haired girls, who'd once fought each other with sword and musket, confronted the monster together.

"So what am I supposed to do?" I called out to them. It would be all right for me to join the conversation now.

"Hm? Well, of course, Kimi—"

"You stay where you are, out of the way."

Oof. Totally not fair.

"—Gugyaaaaaaaaaaaaaaaaaaaaaaaaaaaah!"

Just then, apparently tired of waiting, Betelgeuse gave a roar and charged despite its wounded front leg. Every step made the ground shake.

"Honestly. And I spent so much time training it..." Sighing, Hel had a hand on her saber—then vanished. The very next instant, the red blade slashed at the monster's other front leg.

"What happened to fighting alongside each other?" Siesta grumbled. It would be great if she took this opportunity to understand how I felt.

"If it frustrates you, try to keep up." Hel glanced back at Siesta and smiled.

"...Maybe I'll take you down first after all." But even as she said it, Siesta sprang forward and fired a bullet into the patch of missing scales.

"With that huge body, one shot won't do a thing."

"I don't need you to tell me that."

Sniping at each other, the two of them threw themselves into the battle against the monster. From the sidelines, it almost looked like a fight between sisters. Since they'd inherited DNA from the same parent through their seeds, the two could count as siblings.

"—The same DNA, huh?"

Out of nowhere, I remembered the showdown they'd had on that isolated island last year. At the end of it, Hel had stolen Siesta's heart and transplanted it into her own body. However, Natsunagi's plan had returned it to Siesta. In that case…whose heart was Hel using now?

"——! Gaaaaaaaaaaaaaaaaaaaaaaaaaaaaah!" The monster's scream was high and scratchy.

Dodging and weaving through its multitude of tentacles, Hel and Siesta continued inflicting irreparable damage on Betelgeuse as if this was some sort of competition.

"So, Hel. How exactly are you moving right now?" Keeping her musket trained on the enemy, Siesta glanced at Hel's chest. It was as if she were trying to see the new heart that had to be in there and identify its donor.

"I'm—we're—borrowing *that girl's* life."

"…That girl?" Siesta furrowed her brows. Leaving her behind, Hel darted in close to the enemy.

"—Is that what it is?"

I'd thought of one possibility for the identity of "that girl." She'd undergone clinical trials at SPES's lab, and so she'd acquired the same DNA from Seed as Natsunagi had…

"Will it be a bit quieter now?"

Using slash attacks no ordinary eye could follow, Hel finally brought the monster down. When she returned to stand next to me, my eyes traveled to the left side of her chest. I had a hunch.

"Hel. The heart you have now is Alicia's, isn't it?"

Even before Hel reacted, Siesta's eyes went wide.

Hel blinked slowly, and when her red eyes opened, they were burning with quiet flame. "Yes. Right now, her pulse is what's keeping us alive."

"...Why?" Siesta's blue eyes wavered. "Why Alicia's heart? Six years ago, she—"

Alicia had died protecting Natsunagi and Siesta at the SPES laboratory. ...So what was her heart doing inside Hel?

"She was originally one of Father's vessel candidates as well. As a result, *when that happened*, special measures were taken." Hel relayed information from six years ago, facts she'd learned during her time as a SPES executive. "That day, her body rejected Father's seed and died. However, since she had been a vessel candidate, her *organs* were valuable specimens. Just as your body survived through cryonics, they preserved her heart in a special environment."

When I heard that, I remembered my visit to that laboratory a few days ago. Siesta hadn't been the only one there; Alicia's will had been sleeping there as well.

"Alicia's heart has Seed's DNA. I guess that's why it was a match for you."

Six years ago, at the SPES lab, Siesta, Natsunagi, and Alicia had been told they were participating in clinical trials and given medication. The goal was clear: to prevent their bodies from rejecting Seed if they became his vessel someday. They might have had his cells implanted in them to act as antibodies.

"Yes, exactly. This heart belonged to a twelve-year-old, though. It isn't fully grown yet, which means I can't push myself too much."

...Except Hel had just finished a very dynamic fight.

"As a result, I don't have as much power at my disposal as I used to, but..." Hel was about to continue when her eyes suddenly widened in surprise. She was looking at Siesta, who was crying.

"I'm sorry, Alicia." A single tear trickled from the detective's blue eyes. "Six years ago, I couldn't save you..."

It had happened before she became the Ace Detective. It was her one regret, the one thing she couldn't undo. That day was what had pushed Siesta to start her journey in fighting against the world's enemies.

"I was weak back then. I couldn't protect you—But..." Even though tears were still rolling down her cheeks, Siesta's voice was dignified. "That's not true anymore. I won't let anyone take anything else that's precious to me. I want you to fight beside me again."

The detective extended her left hand to the companion in her distant memories.

"My name is Hel. Code name: Hel. I tell you these words as the queen who rules the land of the dead." Hel looked straight at Siesta. "Thank you for remembering me."

It was the reverse of Alicia's final wish. But I knew Hel had picked up on the voice in her heart and relayed it to Siesta.

Immediately after that, the monster howled again. As if preparing for its final attack, the dozens of tentacles on its back lashed wildly. They'd been shot with the red bullet, though, and they only struck at empty space: Siesta was standing in front of us, and they couldn't attack her.

"This six-year story is about to reach its climax."

"Yes. Let's all end it together."

The white- and black-haired girls stood side by side, one gripping her musket and the other her sword.

It might have been my imagination, but I thought I saw another, smaller form standing between them.

## ◆ The future entrusted to a neighbor

The fight seemed to last an eternity; we couldn't let our guards down for a moment. In terms of actual time, though, the battle didn't even last a few minutes. Finally, with a brief howl from the monster, it was over.

"Did that do it?"

Siesta and Hel were panting, shoulders heaving. As I watched their backs, I uncurled my clenched fists.

"...Hff...hff... Your pet is...far too...undisciplined."

"......! ...Hff. They do say little ones that cause you the most trouble are the cutest."

As they bantered, their eyes were fixed on the shopping mall, which had fused with the huge tree. Betelgeuse was lying at its foot. Siesta's bullets and Hel's slashes had finally made the walking disaster stop moving.

"I was impressed you slid right up to the enemy and hit it with a bullet at the end there."

"Well, I didn't want you to get all the glory."

"You always did hate to lose, hero."

Even as Hel and Siesta argued they exchanged a low-five without turning to face each other. They weren't enemies, and they weren't allies. They'd only shared a common goal temporarily, and their united front had succeeded. But now...

"Be careful," I told them, moving closer. What would happen now that they'd defeated the biological weapon? I knew better than anyone: I'd *taken damage* from it before.

"The pollen."

Siesta narrowed her eyes, gazing into the distance. Large flower buds had begun to sprout from Betelgeuse's corpse. A year ago, after the fight with Hel, I'd been hit by the pollen from those flowers and lost my memories of the previous few hours. I'd forgotten the truth of Siesta's death and the feelings she'd entrusted to me and spent a year soaking in tepid routine.

The same thing was about to happen now. We had to cut down those buds before they opened—

"Something's wrong."

Just as I was about to move, Hel stopped me. The next instant, the buds that had sprouted all over Betelgeuse *began wilting en masse*.

At first, I thought Siesta and Hel had beat Betelgeuse so thoroughly that it no longer had the strength to make them bloom. But when I considered who'd made Betelgeuse in the first place, the answer was obvious.

"—Seed."

Beneath the great tree, an unsteady humanoid silhouette appeared beside the fallen monster.

It was Seed, the parent of all the clones.

The hole in his abdomen was closing, as if the cells were regenerating. A few of his tentacles had crawled over the ground and absorbed energy from Betelgeuse. Seed could share his own power with the pseudohumans, and he could also take it back.

"Father," Hel murmured. Her black hair fluttered in the wind, and I couldn't see her face.

"—Why?" Seed's voice sounded staticky. "Hel, why are you on their side? What's become of your mission? Do you intend to wipe out our seeds?" Seed was seeing his former right-hand woman again for the first time in a year, but he felt nothing. He only spoke to her coldly. "Come fight for me once more."

"That was my plan all along. ...At least, I wish I could tell you it was." Hel took a few steps toward Seed. "Unfortunately, I can't beat this ace detective. I got a good look at her during the fight, and I'm sure of it. As I am now, I can't inflict a single lethal wound on her."

As Hel coolly analyzed the difference in strength between herself and Siesta, her expression softened. She knew better than anyone that she was currently injured.

"Father, we lose." With that, Hel announced the final result of the long battle between SPES and the Ace Detective. She'd determined that Seed couldn't beat Siesta at this point, either.

"—In that case, Hel, become my vessel."

But the answer Seed found was different.

For a moment, all three of us froze up.

"That is your mission and your reason for existing."

...He was right. Hel had originally been a candidate vessel for Seed. Until now, Siesta had been inside her, keeping Seed out, but now that the two of them had separated, Seed would be able to use either one.

"Me, be your vessel, Father...?" Hel's red eyes wavered. Ever since birth— ever since she'd come into being as a new personality inside Natsunagi— Seed's orders had been her only guiding star. To Hel, they had been an absolute, unchanging spell that had bound her. All of her personal principles had been influenced by him.

Now, after a full year, she'd received another mission from Seed. In theory, fighting Siesta and winning was impossible, and she could refuse.

However, it was possible for her to serve as Seed's foundation. So the idea of Hel rejecting Seed's order was—

"I refuse."

Hel wasn't the one who had answered.

Startled, she turned and looked at the white-haired detective.

"Why would you...?" Hel didn't know why Siesta was protecting her. What situation would make shielding her former enemy worth it?

"No idea." Unusually, Siesta's tone was rather childish.

"I don't want that. That's all."

The Siesta who'd operated on logic would have considered that conclusion unreasonable.

But Siesta was familiar with human emotions now.

It had to be because she'd spent the past year in the mind of a girl whose feelings were more passionate than anyone else's.

"—I see."

When Hel heard that, *she smiled*. It wasn't the conniving smile of one forming a plot. Her face was bright, as if a weight had been lifted off her shoulders.

"I'm sorry, Father. Seed, I mean."

Then Hel gave a response to the mission that had been inside her all these years.

"I'm choosing a future in which the people around me will smile."

The saber in Hel's right hand turned toward Seed.

This was the conclusion she'd come to. She'd once agonized over the fact that she was no one, asking herself why she'd been born, but now—in entrusting the proof of her existence to others, she'd found her answer.

To Hel, those "others" were mirrors who would look at the self she wasn't able to see, viewing her from another perspective.

Just as Siesta had tried to protect her from the enemy. Just as Natsunagi had taught her about the passion she'd been unconsciously harboring. Hel had entrusted her course of action to her friends who understood her better than she knew herself.

"Seed. With the sword you gave me, I'll put an end to you."

Hel's red eyes flashed, and those words acquired a soul. It had nothing to do with her seed's ability, though. Hel had vowed to steer this story to its conclusion.

"—So it is as I thought."

Beside Betelgeuse's withering body, Seed took Hel's defection quietly. There was no longer anyone on the battlefield to help him. And yet he was still here. Seed's instinct was to bear descendants; what future would he choose on this battlefield?

"If the parent dies, he can't leave any children." Seed's lightless eyes began to glow dark violet.

"Assistant, are you ready?"

"Yeah. Have been for a year."

It was the beginning of the final battle between SPES and the Ace Detective.

### ◆ The unhappy prince

Seed had declared his intent to fight again, to protect his instinct to leave descendants. He seemed to have finished absorbing the biological weapon's energy; his body bulked up, and thick blood vessels pulsed. Enormous tentacles grew from his shoulders; he reminded me of a Chinese dragon.

"Siesta!" Watching the enemy prepare for war, I gripped my gun. We were past the point where I could afford to be dead weight.

"Yes, let's go."

Siesta and I attacked from his right, while Hel dashed in from the left, holding her saber at waist level. Right now, dealing with those tentacles came first. Splitting up, we each targeted one, and—

"I don't need this right ear anymore."

In the next instant, *Seed's right ear flew off.*

For a brief moment, the sight stopped us in our tracks, but then—

"I won't let you do it."

Realizing what was happening, Siesta fired at Seed.

"That ear had already fulfilled its purpose. It's better to use its energy for other things."

Before Seed had finished speaking, the tentacle growing from his right shoulder morphed into an enormous silver sword and repelled Siesta's bullet.

"Then take this!"

With a loud metallic crash, Hel's red saber knocked the tentacle away. That was all it did, though; she couldn't sever it.

"......!"

The tentacle was even harder than Betelgeuse's scales, and Hel was forced into a one-sided defensive battle.

"Next, my left eye. I don't need it, either." As Seed spoke, the light vanished from his purple eye. "It lost its power seven years ago, in any case."

Then the tentacle on his left shoulder split into a dozen feelers. As if they had wills of their own, they lunged at Siesta.

"—! There's too many of them!"

Siesta tried to fight back with her musket, but even when she shot them off, the countless thin limbs started regenerating in seconds. Like Hel, she was forced to concentrate on defense.

"...So it's down to me, huh?"

With Hel and Siesta pinned, I was the only one left in this fight. Using Chameleon's transformation ability, I blended into the scenery. Seed's right ear had had extremely sharp hearing, just like Bat's. Now that he'd lost that, he wouldn't be able to find me easily. Invisible, I raced toward the enemy.

"And my right eye. I'll discard that as well," Seed murmured while his tentacles kept up their attack. The purple light vanished from his right eye, and—

"......?!"

Just then, the ground jolted under me. *A fissure?* Maybe the seeds he'd sown had sprouted again; I tripped over the cracked ground, and then...

"......! Ghk—Ow..."

A thin briar had sprung up and skewered my right foot.

"Assistant!"

Siesta tried to run to me, but a massive wave of tentacles attacked, blocking her way. Like me, Hel had been trapped by the cracked ground, and she was desperately fighting the silver tentacle.

"...So he doesn't need sight or hearing, huh?"

Using my knife, I cut through the briar, then managed to get back on my feet somehow. In that case... "It's all on you, Siesta."

After all this time, we didn't need words. I just made eye contact with her, then *launched myself* off the asphalt toward a tentacle.

"......!"

A sharp pain ran through my wounded right foot. It didn't matter. Natsunagi must have felt the same fierce agony when she'd faced this enormous evil all by herself.

I pushed through the pain and kept going, using the countless tentacles as footholds. Traveling along a path of tentacles Siesta had made that led to the enemy, I—

"I can catch the scent of human blood no matter where it is."

Just before I reached Seed, a tentacle dug into my side. He'd lost his sight, but Seed's sense of smell was as sharp as Cerberus's, and he'd used that to locate me.

"You are not the one I gave *this* to. I'm reclaiming it."

"....! Gahk—Hah..."

Seed's thin tentacle raked through my insides and pulled *something* out. I spat up dark red blood; my guts were shredded.

"Chameleon's...seed..."

Extracting the black lump that had been buried in me, Seed absorbed it into his own body through his tentacle. I collapsed before I even reached him.

"...! Assistant!"

It was Siesta's voice. She rushed toward me, weaving through the horde of tentacles.

"D-don't."

It was too convenient—my crisis galvanizing Siesta and helping her knock all the tentacles away. If the enemy's attacks had thinned out at a time like this, it meant…

"……Oh."

Maybe it was the effect of the reptile's seed, which he'd taken from me and absorbed. Seed's tentacles had combined into one, and it transformed into a huge snake, sprang at Siesta from behind, and bit her on the neck.

"S-Siesta…"

She collapsed beside me, bleeding all the way from her neck to her shoulders. "…It looks like…I blew it."

"I told you…you freak out too much when I'm in trouble…"

Back when Hel had kidnapped me, Siesta had completely fallen to pieces as she raced to the rescue. The ace detective is usually cool and collected, but whenever this happens, all that goes out the window. Man, I swear…

"…I suspect you like me way too much."

"Are you stupid, Kimi?"

Even as we swapped jokes, we lay on the asphalt, our faces twisted in pain.

"—I knew it." My vision was blurry, but I could see Seed looking down at us with blind eyes. "Because of your emotions, you humans expose yourselves to mortal danger. They threaten your survival instinct. How foolish," he said. There wasn't a trace of anger or pity in his voice. He just spoke coldly, as if he were stating a simple fact.

"You had emotions once too, remember?" I was gritting my teeth so hard I thought they'd shatter as I tried to get up. "You just gave them all away as you made descendants, and then you forgot. Way back when, even you—"

"Yes, that's right. And so the primordial seed *evolved*."

"…?" My mind was becoming hazy from the pain in my side, and I couldn't follow what he was saying.

"When it comes to protecting one's survival instinct, emotions are unnecessary. They are counterproductive, in fact. That is why this body discarded them in the course of its evolution."

…So that was how Seed saw it. Instinct and emotions were different. In fact, emotions threatened the survival instinct, the thing that was most important to Seed... Or to any living creature, actually. As far as he was concerned, losing them was a step in the right direction.

I had no words that could convince him otherwise. If I hadn't been bleeding, if my body had still done what I'd told it to, would I have managed to argue back? ...No, maybe nothing I came up with logically would have worked. What would that girl have done at a time like this? Nagisa Natsunagi, who'd always fought with passion—

"—You haven't lost your emotions yet."

A sharp voice split the air. Still on my knees, I turned to look back. The girl who stood there shared a face with the person I'd been thinking of. She'd stabbed her red sword into the ground and had both hands clasped around its hilt.

"You have one left. Just one."

The uniformed girl was covered in cuts, but she confronted the world's enemy with dignity. Beside her lay the silver tentacle, finally broken.

"What are you talking about?" Seed's blind eyes gazed at Hel.

Biting her lip, Hel spoke about what had happened back then, telling him things even I hadn't known about. "That day, when Nagisa Natsunagi slashed you, you said, 'You too, Hel?' Meaning..." She squeezed the hilt of the saber, the same blade Natsunagi had used that day, and stated her conclusion:

"You were caught off guard by my rebellion, and it made you sad."

The moment Hel said that, Seed's plants all began to wither at once. His sightless eyes widened.

"Our relationship was built on commands. You gave them; I took them. That was all it was." Quietly, Hel described the connection she and Seed had formed over the course of several years. It was similar to the way Siesta and I hadn't been lovers or friends, just odd business partners. "As far as you were concerned, I was a convenient pawn. You didn't tell me what the sacred text really was. I didn't even know you planned to use me as your vessel."

...She was right. When I'd met Hel a year ago, she'd had a blind belief in Seed. As a separate personality that dwelled inside Natsunagi, she'd had no choice. If she hadn't created some sort of bond, she wouldn't have been able to find any meaning in her own existence.

However, when Natsunagi had acquired Siesta's heart, the unconscious Hel had shared memories with Siesta, and she'd realized that Seed had been using her all along.

"I was angry, and I felt betrayed. Maybe that's why I didn't put up much of a fight even after the detective sealed me inside Natsunagi, and why I'm turning my blade on you now that I'm finally free. However..." Hel lowered her saber. "I realized that you and I were the same. I tried to win your trust so that I would have some bond connecting me to this world. In the same way, you really just wanted someone to stay with you."

It had to have been a miscalculation on Seed's part: In order to survive on this planet, he'd gotten too close to mankind. He'd accidentally acquired human emotions, even though they clashed with his survival instinct. But then, in the process of creating pseudohumans, Seed had gradually lost both his power and those feelings.

The emptiness he felt at that loss was far greater than when he'd had nothing to lose. It was like when I'd lost my memories of how Siesta had really died. Or when Siesta had forgotten she'd known Alicia and Natsunagi. Or the way Natsunagi had gone so long without knowing who she was.

Seed was like us. Every time he created a child, he'd lost emotions, and the widening hole in his heart had shocked him more than anyone.

"Father."

Hel called Seed by that name again.

Letting go of her weapon, she took a step closer to him, then another. Her eyes were red and swollen from crying as she shouted, "You trusted me, so I'll say it in your place: Father, you're no monster! *You wanted to be human*; you couldn't possibly be a monster! You've lost your sight, your strength, you've whittled down your life, all to protect your children. The emotion that drove you is called—"

Just then, a tentacle that was no longer silver shot from Seed's right shoulder and pierced Hel's left one.

"——!"

Hel had on a pained expression, but she picked up her saber and cut the tentacle away. "Fa...ther..."

"Don't. That's *no longer Seed*." Siesta squeezed the words out, her hands covering her wounded neck. "His mind has been taken over...by that Ouroboros."

Siesta looked up at the "snake" that had grown from Seed's left shoulder.

"Right ear, left eye, right eye, and then...your mind."

In a voice like low static, the *serpent spoke*. It was as if it had erased what little awareness and emotions Seed had left and now was in control. "Ouroboros" was the name of Seed's survival instinct itself.

"–Blood. There's not enough blood."

Seed's head hung limply. In his place, Ouroboros's golden eyes turned to glare at us.

"Assistant..."

"Siesta..."

Siesta and I reached out for each other. Neither of us was able to stand yet.

".......Ghk."

Hel stood in front, shielding us. Ouroboros sprang at her, baring its huge poisonous fangs—and just as my hazy eyes saw a spray of blood, I blacked out.

## ◇ The tale of the happy swallow

I was deep, deep in the light.

I turned my face away, squeezed my eyes shut, but the light was so bright, it seemed to penetrate through my eyelids.

I was born as a terribly nebulous being: the second personality of a girl. That girl—my master—had been physically frail since she was small and had created me in an attempt to escape the pain of her medical treatments.

As I shared my master's suffering, I hugged my knees, locked away in a world that held no one but me. Still, what I found hardest to bear was the "light" the girl radiated.

That smile, bright as the summer sun. The only reason she could smile like that was because I was bearing half her pain for her, but as she talked cheerfully with her friends, she had no idea. I couldn't have hated her more.

We were two sides of the same coin, though, and one day, we finally switched places.

"*Your name is Hel. Code name: Hel.*"

When I opened my eyes, the first voice I heard was Seed's.

My name was Hel.

Code name: Hel.

When he called my name—when I, who was no one, had my existence recognized—it felt as if a ray of darkness had appeared in the light. I couldn't imagine anything more pleasant than the chill of that darkness.

"You have a mission. In order to protect your comrades, destroy the world." With that, Seed had handed me a book.

"Destroying the world is my duty?"

"Destroying the world is our method."

I cocked my head, puzzled, and Seed—Father—went on.

"You have only one duty. No matter what happens, your duty is to survive."

Looking back, maybe Father only said that in order to make his plan a reality. A plausible white lie so that he'd be able to use me as his vessel someday.

Still, when he said them, a certain emotion settled within me. I'd acquired a bond that let me experience a desire to live. As a result, I began to destroy the world in accordance with the book. Later on, I would learn that it was a book of prophecies known as "the sacred text."

"I know this isn't right."

Even as I told myself that, I swung the red sword Father had given me.

I thought things were best this way. A single black drop had fallen into that dazzling light, and I clung to the stain. If doing so would get this world, and Father, to acknowledge me... If my mission was to be the world's enemy, then I'd live for that alone.

If I'd made one miscalculation, it was this: Although I'd hated that light and my master more than anything, somewhere along the way, I'd begun to treasure them. That hesitation and weakness *had created this battlefield*, and the thought made me smile bitterly at my own pathetic weakness.

"—No. It wasn't 'somewhere along the way.'"

It had been like that all along. Nagisa and I were two sides of the same coin, a reflection in a mirror.

My envy had belied my affection.

"Are you still alive?"

I'd fallen to my knees. Far overhead, the golden eyes of Ouroboros looked down at me. This was Father's survival instinct, its physical manifestation. Did this mean I would have to cut off its head before anything I said could reach him?

"Will you get up again? Will you give me more blood?"

The snake coiled in midair, and its red tongue flicked. My blood contained Father's DNA; it probably wanted to absorb it and build up its strength.

"Don't misunderstand, all right?"

Stabbing my saber into the ground to use as a support, I got to my feet. How could I go back into combat against it? How could I stand up again? Apparently, the snake didn't know. Well, it was only instinct, with no memories or emotions, so there was probably no help for that.

That person had definitely said it, though:

"Father ordered me to live, no matter what."

*Sorry, but I promised.* Leveling the red sword Father had given me, I charged at the enemy dominating the space under the great tree.

"Don't worry, Father. You don't have to do this anymore. Your first survival instinct has already been satisfied."

Slashing through the briars that sprang up from the ground to attack me, I ran toward him.

He was still unconscious on his feet. Most of his armor had crumbled, and there were cracks in his body. His eyes were blind, and I didn't know whether his remaining ear could hear. He'd lost his awareness and his emotions. He was simply waiting to dry up and wither away. Even so, I shouted at him.

"What you wanted to leave behind is alive on this planet! The sapphire eye, the ruby sword, a heart of lead—All of them are here!"

Pseudohumans weren't the only things Father had left in this world.

A sapphire eye that could see through anything, even human hearts.

A ruby-colored sword lit with the flames of passion.

A heart of lead that hadn't broken, even after death.

Father must have wanted to protect all those things, really.

"—The ears that could have heard you are already gone."

The tail of Ouroboros whipped toward me, slicing through the wind. I was sure I saw the snake smirk at me, but in the next moment, its golden eyes widened in surprise.

That attack had been aimed at my heart, but it stopped dead just before it reached my chest.

Why hadn't the blade touched me? *Exactly who had stopped it?* I didn't even have to explain.

"The survival instinct you always prioritized will remain on this planet as your undying legacy: the *love* that protected your children to the end! That last wish will never die!"

That had to be the true essence of the primordial seed's first survival instinct.

The name of the emotion that Father had lost long ago.

"......! You stay out of this...!"

Ouroboros glared at its host. I was only a few meters away by then, and it struck at me with its enormous fangs. I parried with my saber, and the blow knocked me back a good distance.

"...Maybe I pushed myself a bit too hard."

I'd been thrown onto the concrete. When I tried to get up, my strength failed me, and I dropped to my knees. I hadn't had Alicia's heart for very long—and only a few days ago, this body had basically been dead. The fact that I'd gotten back up at all should have counted as a miracle.

"—Ha...ha-ha." The snake laughed, as if it were eating away at the faint traces of emotion it had absorbed from Father. "Those who've violated the principles of life have no right to live again—or to defy this survival instinct."

Then Ouroboros gave a great howl. It attacked with its poisonous fangs again, and again I was thrown back.

"Sorry, Hel. I overslept."

...But it was the detective's assistant who'd thrown me off this time.

"That's just what I'd expect from my partner. You came to save me." With an intentionally fake smile, I let him help me up.

Then I heard a gunshot. The detective had also woken from her nap and was battling Ouroboros with her musket.

"Sheesh. You two aren't exactly unscathed either, you know." I sighed, looking at the boy; he was bleeding from his forehead and stomach.

"Yeah. Well, you know, I couldn't keep that promise." He bit his lip.

Promise. No doubt he meant the one he'd made to me a few days earlier, while he was carrying Nagisa Natsunagi piggyback at the laboratory. If he did anything to make my master cry—I'd kill him twice.

Did that mean he was trying to protect her through me now? If so...

"That promise will never expire. Stay by my master from now on." I gripped my red sword again, turning to look at the enemy.

"—You're going?" Realizing what I was about to attempt, the boy held me back for a moment.

"Yes. You should go to your partner, too. I'm sure she could use some help."

"...Yeah. But you're..."

His eyes were damp, to my surprise.

He couldn't be feeling sympathy for *me, the enemy*, could he? If he was, I felt like I might laugh just a little... But no, it wasn't funny. I hoped his indecisiveness wouldn't hold him back... But we could deal with that by having his *partner* train him properly. I started toward the primordial seed again and turned back to the boy one more time.

"I'm glad I was born."

When I said it, for a moment, his eyes widened in surprise. Then he gave a soft smile.

Why had I wanted to tell him that now? I wasn't sure, but my heart was calm.

"Take care of my master, Kimihiko Kimizuka." With his name as my final words, I ran like the wind.

On the way, my eyes met the white-haired girl's blue ones.

A year ago, I'd asked the pair of enemies who stood in my way how they could trust each other so much. I'd been sealed within my master's body before I'd managed to understand their relationship. Now, though, I understood. No... They'd told me as much back then.

"It was their bond."

Ouroboros's tail was right in front of me, and as I murmured those words to myself, I unconsciously cut it off with the *shining red sword*. Exchanging one last, wordless look with the Ace Detective, I launched myself off the ground.

"This is how she and I should be."

*Maybe it's another sort of bond—although that would be wrapping things up too neatly*, I thought, smiling wryly.

In the end, at the very least, I'd formed a bond with Nagisa Natsunagi. Now I had to tell Father about it. That was my final mission.

*"My legs will not stop."*

Using my word-soul ability, I gave myself an order. In response, the sword in my hands blazed red. I'd channeled all of my seed's power, and even my own mind, into that red sword. Then I'd use it to destroy the primordial seed itself—the Ouroboros was bound to die as well. I ran toward Seed on legs that would never stop.

Father was at the foot of the building that had been pierced by the tree. That tree had grown even bigger; by now, it had almost swallowed the fifty-meter building.

"I will take responsibility for all our crimes."

The wounds we'd inflicted on this world would never fully heal.

Shouldering all the sins, the bloodshed, and the weight of life, I ran across the battlefield.

All the cells in my body. The power of the seed engraved in each cell. My own consciousness. I focused all of these in the palm of my hand, channeling them into the ruby sword.

"I believe that this was love."

And then...

"Hel...!"

With Kimihiko Kimizuka yelling behind me, I ran my sword through the primordial seed's stomach.

"Aaaaaaaaaaaaaaaaaaaaaaaaaaaaaaah!"

What was this emotion?

It wasn't anger or sadness—but I had to scream. I couldn't help it.

With the strength that could have shattered all the bones in my body, I impaled Seed with my sword and pinned him to the towering tree.

"——! Hah..."

A small groan escaped Father's lips, just above my head.

At the same time, I heard the monster's dying shrieks behind me.

Our final enemy had just perished.

"—H...Hel?"

I heard a familiar, beloved voice.

It was the voice that had given me my name six years ago.

"Yes. Code name: Hel. I'm right here." I responded just as I had on that day, but the answer I gave was different. "Father, let's go home. Back to the world where we belong."

When I looked up—Was it my imagination? I thought his lips held the faint suggestion of a smile.

"...Yes. I am a little tired."

Father sounded almost like an ordinary human, and his words were the last thing I heard. Falling against his chest, I slowly, slowly closed my eyes.

# Chapter 2

## ◆ Epilogue and Prologue

*"I see. So one global crisis has ended."*

On the other end of the line, the girl gave a relieved sigh.

"Yeah. It's been a week, but apparently the seal on Seed is holding." In the corridor of a certain small hospital, I leaned against the wall.

One week ago, we'd tackled a worldwide calamity in that city taken over by plants. Siesta, Hel, and I had fought Seed; we'd ultimately won but at a heavy cost.

Hel, Nagisa Natsunagi's second personality, had infused the red sword with her own mind and the power of the seed inside her and sealed them into the tree with Seed. That tree still towered there, like a watchtower over mankind.

*"Excellent work, Kimihiko,"* said the girl on the phone. *"You chose a route for the future that even I couldn't foresee, and you saved the world magnificently. As a Tuner, you have my gratitude. Thank you."*

Even through the call, and the nine thousand kilometers between us, I could tell she was bowing.

"...I didn't do anything."

It was true that one global crisis was over, but I hadn't been the one to end it. The sacrifices of Siesta, Natsunagi, and many of our comrades had done that. And finally, it had been Hel who'd put Seed to sleep with the passion she'd inherited from her master.

Had she been happy in the end? I thought about it as I gazed at the great tree. The dead can't talk, which is why the living should respect that silence. We shouldn't speak on their behalf.

*Even so*, I thought in spite of myself. Hel's life had been a constant search for love. I couldn't help but hope she'd sleep peacefully in the shelter of that tree with Seed, who had finally learned—or rather, remembered— what it meant to feel emotion.

"You're the one who really had it rough, Mia," I said, shifting the topic to something else.

As the Oracle, Mia's Tuner role was to foresee the world's crises, and she'd helped Siesta fight against Seed for years. She might have even more history with him than I did. Now that their score was finally settled, she'd returned to that clock tower in London.

"*So did you. And? How are your injuries?*"

"Oh, I'm well enough to talk on the phone."

That said, Seed's tentacle had ripped into my side. I could easily still have been hovering between life and death. The effects of the seed I'd swallowed seemed to have lingered, though. Thanks to its astonishing powers of recovery, the wound had almost healed over. Seed might have extracted it, but, for better or for worse, maybe some of its effects would stick around. More importantly, right now...

"If I had to say, Siesta took more damage."

On the battlefield, Ouroboros had bitten Siesta's neck and inflicted a large wound. She'd been transported to this hospital, and as of today, she'd finally recovered enough to be allowed to have visitors. The fact that it required some time to heal despite Siesta's unusually strong powers of recovery showed how bad the bite had actually been.

"*I imagine she'll heal more quickly if you pay her a visit, then. Through the power of love, you know,*" Mia joked.

"Is that another prophecy?"

"*Women's intuition.*"

...Oh, is that right? Telling her I'd see her later, I hung up.

When I reached Siesta's hospital room, I took a deep breath outside the door.

I'd just reunited with my former partner after a year apart, and due to the situation, we hadn't been able to really talk before. Now that we did have the time, what should we talk about? What should I tell her? I couldn't gather my thoughts properly, but I opened the door anyway.

"Hey, how are you feeling?"

For a private room, it was pretty big.

The Ace Detective was sitting up in the bed by the window, dressed in a hospital gown.

"I can't believe you recovered first. I must be losing my touch." Siesta turned to look at me. The morning sun's light shone against her pale silver hair, and she had on a playful smile. I didn't know if you could call this "fine," but she was feeling well enough to kid around, at least.

"Charlie's here too, huh?" I spotted the blond agent in a chair near the bed. She must have come to visit Siesta, but she was heavily bandaged herself. "...? What's up, Charlie?"

Charlie still hadn't spoken. She seemed restless; she kept stealing glances at Siesta, then letting her gaze fall to her hands. She'd always been really attached to the detective. I wouldn't have been surprised if she threw her arms around Siesta in joy, but...

"Yes, that's what I expected too at first." Realizing what I was actually asking, Siesta answered for Charlie. "Apparently seeing me again for the first time in so long has made her shy, and she doesn't know how she should act around me."

"M-Ma'am! Please don't say it!" Charlie kept her eyes riveted on her knees, but her face flushed apple red.

"Charlie, are you a lovestruck maiden or something?"

"Sh-shut up. You know I can't help it." Whatever this was, she had it bad. Even when she snapped at me, her heart wasn't in it. "I mean, I had no idea a miracle like this could happen. ...Well, of course I believed, and I planned to do what had to be done. Now that it's actually come true, though, I don't know what to do...," she murmured softly, clenching her fists.

"Come here."

Watching her beloved apprentice, Siesta spoke to her gently. Charlie's shoulders flinched, and she slowly looked up.

"I'm sorry for making you sad." Apologizing to Charlie the same way she'd apologized to me, she gently stroked her head.

"......Mgh. Ma'am, Ma'am...!"

Charlie's eyes opened wide, filled with tears. She clung to Siesta, crying like a child.

"Yeesh. Just be honest about this stuff to begin with, wouldja?" After I'd watched them for a little while, I smiled wryly and went to change the flowers in the vase by the window.

"...You're the last person I want to hear that from, Kimizuka." Charlie's sharp ears had caught my murmur; she poked her head out from within Siesta's arms and glared at me.

"You two haven't changed a bit. Can't you get along a little better than that?"

"There will never be a day when Kimizuka and I get along!" Resting her head on Siesta's lap, Charlie started insulting me.

"I thought we'd started to understand each other a little."

"It's possible to understand something logically and still be physically unable to stomach it."

"Sorry, Siesta. I guess we're exactly where we were a year ago."

If this incident hadn't been enough to bring us closer, it was never gonna happen. Sighing, I sat down on a stool near the bed.

"Heh-heh!" Unexpectedly, Siesta's lips softened into a smile. She stroked Charlie's hair. "It's okay. It's been a long time since I got to see both of you doing your banter routine."

""It's not a routine, Ma'am!""

Charlie and I spoke in unison, then glared at each other.

In the middle of our mudslinging contest...

"I really wish you wouldn't hold these fun little parties without me!"

It was an idol with pink and white streaks in her hair and an eye patch over her left eye: Yui Saikawa had arrived.

"Yui!" Charlie sat up with relief. ...But her gaze was focused on Saikawa at a lower angle than usual.

"Hey there. You okay now?"

"I'm just perfect! ...Actually, that would be a bit of an overstatement,

but I'm doing well!" *From her wheelchair,* Saikawa flashed us a peace sign. Her legs were fine, but she wasn't strong enough to walk yet. Noches, the maid formerly known as SIESTA, was pushing the wheelchair. She'd been taking care of everyone for the past week.

"You always look so at home in that maid uniform."

"And you always notice the same things, Kimihiko."

I see. I knew she wasn't complimenting me.

While Noches and I were talking…

"This is the first time we've met in person, isn't it?" From the bed, Siesta gave Saikawa a gentle smile.

"It's nice to meet you, Siesta. I'm Yui Saikawa, the world's cutest idol!" From her wheelchair, Saikawa gave her very best elevator pitch. Siesta had known about Saikawa and had been working to protect her from the shadows, but this was their first time meeting each other in person.

"I'm told I caused you a lot of trouble. I'm sorry." A slight shadow fell across Saikawa's smile, and she bowed her head. Saikawa's parents had once funded SPES's activities.

"It's nothing you need to apologize for, Yui." Siesta stroked Saikawa's hair. "And thank you for staying with my assistant while I was gone."

"Siesta…" The two of them locked eyes, and then… "Yes, honestly, taking care of Kimizuka was an awful lot of work. I massaged him, I cooked for him… He may not look it, but he can be quite a baby. There were times when I had to hold him tightly…"

"Quit making stuff up."

"Ow!"

I karate chopped Saikawa's head. Her eyes teared up. "But I wasn't…" Her mumbling didn't make much sense to me, though. Siesta gave me a cold look, and I got the feeling she'd muttered a certain word starting with "p," but since there was some conveniently loud construction work going on outside, I didn't catch it.

"Still, I see." Siesta's eyes softened, and she looked at me. "So these are your current companions, Kimi."

In addition to Siesta, there was Saikawa, Charlie, and Noches present in the room. And although they weren't physically here, Mia and the red-headed policewoman probably counted, too.

Compared to a few years ago, I definitely had more friends and gained more precious things. Right now, I'm able to think that from the bottom of my heart...or I should have been. However, there was one person who wasn't here, so I shook my head.

"There's one more. If we left her out, she'd be madder than anyone." When they heard that, Saikawa and Charlie both looked down.

Nagisa Natsunagi.

Alicia's heart had been transplanted successfully, and the primordial seed's order had brought her out of her dormant state. Then, during that final showdown, Hel had permanently sealed her own mind. It wouldn't have been odd for Natsunagi's personality to wake up and take her place.

But a week had passed, her injuries had been thoroughly treated, and she still wouldn't wake up. She was asleep in a different hospital room all by herself.

"I haven't forgotten her, of course. I couldn't possibly forget," Siesta said. Her eyes were closed.

However, when she opened them, she said:

"And so, Assistant, let's go on a journey to save our friend."

She held out her left hand to me.

"But how?" Was there anything we could do?

As I hesitated, Siesta said, "There's someone we still need to meet and talk to."

...Oh, right. That individual was deeply involved with our current situation, but he hadn't yet made an appearance. Over the past week, I'd tried to make contact with him several times, but he'd never shown himself.

From the way Siesta was talking, though, a meeting had been arranged. There were a ton of things we'd have to discuss with him.

"In that case, if you're ready, shall we go see him?" Even though Siesta was still on bed rest, she sat up as she spoke. "...The underground doctor who saved all our lives."

## ◆ He who protects the living

After I'd helped Siesta into a wheelchair, we headed for another hospital room. We hadn't wanted to barge in as a crowd, so the two of us went on behalf of our group.

We made our way down the dingy corridor of the little hospital, and when we opened the door of that room—we saw a girl lying on the only bed.

"Natsunagi..."

Pushing Siesta's wheelchair, I went closer.

I'd visited this room several times in the past week, but I still hadn't gotten to see Natsunagi smile like she used to.

"The conditions for Nagisa to awaken seem to be in place." From the wheelchair, Siesta gazed at her, analyzing the situation. "All that's left are the things we *amateurs* can't pick up on. Whether there's serious internal damage, for example. Say she managed to miraculously overcome brain death by going dormant. It's still possible that it put too much stress on her cerebrum, and she's fallen into a vegetative state."

"Yeah, that's about all I can think of, too. I spent the past week reading through all the medical journals I could find, but an amateur who's studying this stuff on the fly was never going to come up with a great theory anyway. Besides, since Natsunagi's a special case, previous case studies probably won't be much help."

That was exactly why we needed a *specialist* right now. This medical expert had saved Natsunagi's life once; he might know what it would take to wake her up again.

"Before you worry about others, you should remember that you're badly injured yourselves."

★  ★  ★

A man spoke behind us. I turned around…but he didn't even glance at me. Instead, he walked straight to Natsunagi.

"She's making good progress. It appears there were no real problems while I was away," the man murmured in a rather monotone voice, adjusting the IV drip in Natsunagi's arm.

"Thanks for all your help," I told him, and he finally turned to look at us across the bed. He seemed to be in his midthirties. He had bright blond hair, but the eyes behind his round glasses were of a subdued color. Even at a glance, you could see his intelligence in his features, and in his lab coat, he looked like a knowledgeable researcher as well as a doctor.

"Do you mean with this girl? Or are you referring to yourself? I've taken care of more patients than I can count, so there are far too many cases you could be referring to."

It sounded like a joke, but the man spoke in a matter-of-fact way, and his expression didn't change. I guess I should've known he wouldn't be the type to crack jokes.

"I meant both of us. And Siesta, Saikawa, and Charlie, too, actually… You helped all of them as well. I'm grateful."

I didn't just mean this time, either. I'd been brought here when I was wounded in our previous battle with Seed, and this doctor had treated me then, too. He was the director of the hospital and the man I'd asked about Natsunagi's condition.

From what I'd heard, this hospital didn't take ordinary patients. It existed to treat people in special situations like ours. During the three years we'd spent traveling, both Siesta and I had been saved by back-alley doctors like this one time and time again.

"No, there's no need for gratitude. It's my job—and the duty I must fulfill in this world."

…The conversation was oddly failing to connect. It was as if none of his words were allowed to leave any room for interpretation. He seemed to be refusing to read between the lines, or to let us do it.

"I suppose I haven't introduced myself." The man didn't bother to read the mood or pick the correct moment, and his face stayed blank.

"I am Stephen Bluefield—the Inventor."

*The Inventor.* When I heard that, the first thing I thought of was Thomas Edison, the world-famous king of inventions. If you went back in time a bit, there was also Hiraga Gennai of Japan, inventor of the electrostatic generator. However, the man probably wasn't talking about *ordinary inventors like those.*

"He's a Tuner," Siesta chimed in; she'd been listening quietly up till now. "He was involved in the manufacture of my Seven Tools as well. He preserved my body cryogenically in suspended animation, and he also equipped it with an AI and created Noches—He's the Inventor, an underground doctor."

...So I'd been right about that. Two weeks ago, I'd had missed the chance to meet him at the SPES hideout. Although I hadn't seen him then, this guy was the unknown doctor who'd based himself within the lab. He was a Tuner, one of the world's twelve guardians.

"It's been a long time, Stephen." Siesta looked up at him from her wheelchair.

These Tuners seemed to have a lot of shared history I didn't know about.

"Yes. Seeing you moving and talking this way makes it clear that the yearlong course of experimental treatment was a success." Gazing at the patient for whom he'd done so much for so long, Stephen smiled a little.

Siesta told him, "You and Nagisa saved my life. But, Stephen, if you consider it your mission to save lives, then please: I want you to save Nagisa this time."

She was asking Stephen for help again, in order to repay the debt she owed Natsunagi. She believed this man was the only one who could possibly know how to wake her up.

"Daydream." Stephen called Siesta by her nickname as he entered notes into a patient chart. "You're drastically *underestimating* my skills as a physician."

That didn't seem right. Shouldn't it have been "overestimating"?

He wasn't being modest and telling her he didn't have that kind of power.

"In order to save my patients—my *clients*—I always do everything I can. I pour my heart's blood into the work and call upon all the knowledge and technical skill I possess. If the patient fails to wake up even then, I never blame myself. I'm aware that I've already done all that could be done."

There was no anger or dissatisfaction in his voice. He was just telling us the cold, hard facts, and Siesta and I listened.

"If there was anything I could still do for a patient, it would be proof that I had previously cut corners. As a Tuner and a doctor, I take pride in my principles, so I assure you, I've done everything I could."

At that point, I understood why Ms. Fuubi had told me *"Nagisa Natsunagi is dead"* that day. She made that statement due to the trust she placed in the Inventor.

Ms. Fuubi had to be familiar with Stephen Bluefield's personal philosophy. When he'd performed treatment and gave the diagnosis of brain death, she'd understood there was nothing more that could be done.

"That other time, too. So that's why..."

Come to think of it, when I'd sworn to bring Siesta back to life a few weeks ago, Fuubi had hinted at a possibility by telling me about Mia Whitlock, the Oracle. Putting us in contact with Stephen should have been the more natural thing to do, since the Inventor had been involved in Siesta's treatment.

But Ms. Fuubi hadn't done that. She knew that the Inventor had already done his best, so there was nothing left for him to do. Still, I believed in miracles, and so she'd introduced me to the Oracle; she hadn't had any other leads.

"Therefore, there's nothing else I can do for Nagisa Natsunagi." Telling us bluntly that the current treatment was the final option, Stephen briskly turned and left the hospital room, white coat flaring behind him. He'd been gone this whole week; he might be on his way to see another patient with special circumstances.

"Wait." Siesta rolled her wheelchair after Stephen. Following them out to the corridor, I saw the Inventor had stopped. He still had his back to her.

"I know about your philosophies, too," Siesta told him. "You have another one: You refuse to attempt surgeries that are one hundred percent impossible. Meaning that if you were to get involved, there's a definite chance that that patient will be saved."

It was the Inventor's second conviction. Siesta was insisting since that was the case, there must still be at least a 1 percent chance that Natsunagi would wake up.

"You diagnosed Nagisa as brain-dead, and you donated her heart to me in accordance with her wishes. But you didn't stop there."

She was right: Stephen had transplanted Alicia's heart into Natsunagi. Ordinarily, brain-dead patients had no chance of recovery. Even so, Stephen had conducted the second transplant; that had to mean he'd seen a possibility of at least 1 percent.

"On that day," Stephen began, still with his back to us, "after Nagisa was declared brain-dead, I did transplant her heart into you. As a doctor, it was my job to do so. However..." He turned to face us. "After that, I did my job as an inventor."

The hint of a smile in his blue eyes was unsettling.

"I hate miracles that can't be reproduced."

His expression promptly reverted to the chilly, intelligent one he'd worn earlier.

"Ordinary humans don't come back to life. I'm aware of that. Still, I was exceedingly conscious of the fact that your bodies are not normal." As Stephen spoke, he was gazing at Siesta—or possibly at the left side of her chest. "I was also intrigued by the primordial seed that made you this way."

"Is that why you worked out of the SPES lab for so long?"

When Natsunagi and I visited the place two weeks ago, Noches had mentioned that Stephen was researching the primordial seed there while he continued Siesta's treatment.

"That's right. As a matter of fact, when the Daydream died a year ago, I preserved her body with cryonics...but the operation didn't succeed through my skill alone. Immediately after death, she made an involuntary attempt to preserve her life by going dormant."

Glancing at Siesta, he gave us additional information about how she'd resurrected.

"Then, as I was performing Nagisa's surgery, I had a sudden revelation: As the sole fully compatible host for the primordial seed, she might have done the same and intentionally put herself into suspended animation."

That was what had led Stephen to help Natsunagi a second time, even though she was supposed to be dead.

"That is why, after I had transplanted her heart into you, I transplanted the girl Alicia's heart into her. I was concerned Nagisa's heart might be too damaged for the procedure, so I had brought a spare from the laboratory—and it proved to be the right choice."

"So that's why Alicia's heart was here...," Siesta murmured.

The medication trials she, Natsunagi, and Alicia had undergone six years ago had given them DNA from Seed. That was why their three hearts were *interchangeable* and why the surgeries had been a success.

"Both operations, including the transplants themselves, succeeded without incident. However, neither you nor Nagisa awakened immediately. In particular, Nagisa showed no vital reactions that would overturn my diagnosis of brain death, and the limit seemed to be drawing near. That was when you happened to visit her hospital room," Stephen told me. I remembered taking Natsunagi's steadily cooling hand about ten days ago.

"Therefore, I did not retract my diagnosis of brain death, and I felt that was the natural result. If this was a world where the dead could be revived so easily, there would be no need for doctors."

He had a point. In terms of modern medicine, Natsunagi had died then. However, three days after that, Stephen had changed his opinion. On that day, one week ago, Siesta had awakened, and Hel had come back to life soon after. Over the course of three days, the heart that had been Siesta's to begin with had settled into her body, and Seed's order had awakened Natsunagi from suspended animation.

"I hate thoughtless words like 'miracle,'" Stephen said again. "Why don't miracles occur consistently? It's illogical. I only believe in things that can be repeated. On that point, since the primordial seed has brought two humans back from the dead, it should be referred to as a reproducible *philosopher's stone*."

"Then there could be a miracle that would wake Natsunagi again…" But even as I said it, I spotted the problem.

The primordial seed himself was already lost. Besides—

"There isn't a fragment of the seed left in Nagisa's body. I've done all I can for *an ordinary human*."

The argument had come full circle: Both as a doctor and an inventor, Stephen had already performed his duty to the best of his abilities. Now he was off to save some other patient with special circumstances somewhere else—leaving Natsunagi behind.

"You used Alicia's life…!"

My strangled voice echoed in the corridor.

He'd used Alicia's heart, her life.

What if, after all that, Natsunagi never woke up? That couldn't possibly be okay.

"Assistant." Siesta gently tugged the cuff of my sleeve. My fists were clenched, and my nails were biting into my palms. One other problem had crossed my mind.

…I knew Stephen had used Alicia's heart to save Natsunagi, as a doctor. But naturally, Alicia's will hadn't been involved. Had it really been the right thing to do? I couldn't—

"It isn't my job to speak for the dead." At the sound of Stephen's voice, I looked up. "The dead cannot speak for themselves. That being the case, my mission is to save the life in front of me. To help people through science. There can't be anything more to it."

I knew that. Just guessing what someone would have wanted and then actually wishing for it on their behalf would be arrogance on the part of the living.

However, an idol had curtailed the debate with pretty words once; she'd worn a nice dress and argued against the skepticism with a song. I didn't know whether that had been right or not.

—Still. If the dead can't talk, it means the question doesn't exist, either. If there's no question, then maybe there never was a correct answer.

"Let me make this clear, Kimihiko Kimizuka." Stephen said my full name, even though I'd never told him what it was. "If it means I will save two people, I will kill one. I can't save all three. Always think of the whole, the greatest good. Numbers are everything. Whatever saves the greatest number of people is the right thing to do. I work to save the living, and I have no time to consider the last wishes of the dead. My next patient is waiting." With that, Stephen left.

In response...Alicia's and Natsunagi's smiling faces came to mind, and I couldn't respond at all.

"Let's go back." Siesta tugged gently on my cuff again. I nodded wordlessly, then returned to the door of Natsunagi's room, which we'd left standing open.

"Sorry to make you listen to all that, Natsunagi," I told her sleeping form. I reached for her hand...but somehow I couldn't bring myself to take it. I felt as if I didn't have the right, considering how we still haven't found a way to wake her up.

"...Hm? What's this?"

I noticed there was something that looked like an old book sitting on a nearby shelf. It was close to the spot where Stephen had first stood.

"......! That's—" Siesta's blue eyes wavered, and I handed her the book. When she opened it...the inside seemed to be a child's picture journal. In the photo, a girl with black hair was sitting on a bed, chatting with a girl with white hair and another with pink hair who stood near her.

"It's Alicia's diary," Siesta murmured. She gently hugged the book to her chest as if it were precious.

"...So we already had our answer." When I saw Alicia's journal and Siesta's profile, I remembered.

Alicia's heart had awakened Natsunagi's body once. I'd seen the three young girls standing side by side. That was the answer. Even if it was a selfish wish, I decided to believe in that sight and in the words Hel had left behind.

"Hurry and wake up, Natsunagi," I told the girl on the bed.

*And then let's have another stupid fight, like we always do.*

## ◆ A journey to foretell the world

Three days passed. During that time, Siesta, Saikawa, Charlie, and I all brainstormed ways to wake Natsunagi up.

Stephen, her attending physician, had already washed his hands of the matter. He'd said something to the effect that there was nothing else he could do, but that didn't necessarily mean there was actually nothing that could be done, period.

Working on that assumption, Siesta named an expert who could step in for the Inventor, and we decided that she and I would go find him right away. However...

"Say, can I order a snack?" Next to me, Siesta was holding an in-flight menu.

I never imagined she'd drag me onto an airplane the day after we got discharged from the hospital...

"They're expensive, so no. I told you to buy something at the kiosk, remember?"

"What could I do? That trouble on the train made us get there at the very last minute. And it was mostly your fault, Kimi."

Siesta's apathetic eyes fixed on me. *Sorry, but if you're going to hang out with me, you're going to get dragged into random trouble. Did she forget about that?*

"Still." Siesta gazed at me and shifted the conversation to something else. "It's been a long time since the two of us were on a plane together, hasn't it?"

We were currently cruising at ten thousand meters aboveground. This was how I'd met Siesta on that fateful day four years ago.

"Yeah. There's no telling how many planes I rode with you after that."

"We racked up an unbelievable number of frequent-flyer miles, didn't we?"

Remembering those three years, we both laughed a little.

Today, we were bound for New York. In order to meet a certain person, and attend *a certain council*, we were globe-trotting for the first time in a year.

"Are you really okay to travel, though?" I asked her again. She'd been injured worse than I had, but she'd left the hospital and boarded the plane as soon as she was able to walk.

"Yes, I'd like to hurry a bit."

"Yeah. Both for Natsunagi and that council." I followed up with a question about one of our objectives. "And? What is this Federal Council, exactly?"

The Federal Council—Siesta had asked me to accompany her to a meeting of all the world's Tuners. The council was apparently held at random locations as needed; it would be in New York this time, and since the Ace Detective was a Tuner, Siesta had an obligation to attend.

"In simple terms, it's a place where the twelve Tuners meet and talk whenever the world has reached a major turning point." As Siesta answered, she was nibbling on a long, thin chocolate snack. When had she bought those? "When a new global crisis is looming, they decide who's going to handle it. Since the 'primordial seed' crisis has passed this time, I suppose there'll be a postmortem report on that as well."

"I see. So you'll be reporting your achievements as the Ace Detective, huh?" From what I was hearing, it sounded as if we'd be the highlight of this conference, in a way. ...Still, meeting in person in this day and age made them seem like a pretty old-fashioned crowd.

"Are you nervous?"

"I'm shaking from excitement."

"Literally, it appears."

*You try getting dumped straight into a massively important discussion that's going to determine the future.*

"Well, there'll be plenty of people you know there. Like her, for example."

"Oh, Ms. Fuubi? Yeah, I'd wondered how you two knew each other. I never figured it'd be this, though."

After the hijacking four years ago, Siesta had handed Bat over to Ms. Fuubi. They'd been connected before I was even aware of it, comrades who protected the world from the shadows.

"So will Mia be there, too?"

"That's a good question. She's never attended before."

True, it was hard to picture a homebody like Mia attending such a tense meeting. Come to think of it, Ms. Fuubi had said she'd never met the Oracle.

"Then you mean people are allowed to skip this thing?" A council that predicted the way of the world seemed like it would be pretty uptight, but...

"All the Tuners besides me have a quirk or two. Not many of them are good at getting along with others."

"You make it sound like you're normal or something."

Siesta only sipped her tea, acting as if she had no idea what I was talking about. *You just brought your own teacup on board like it's nothing.*

"Still, the one we're going to meet is probably the most troublesome member of the group."

...Right. There was another reason we were headed to New York and attending the council.

"The Vampire—Scarlet," I muttered.

Siesta gave a small nod. "You know him already, don't you?"

"Not that I particularly want to see him..."

Even among the Tuners, the Vampire was a heretic. I'd sensed something fathomless in his sharp eyes, which seemed to take the measure of everything. He'd also hinted that there was something between him and Siesta...

"You're acting as if something unpleasant happened. Did he pick on you?"

"...He was just sort of creepy. Never mind that; you really think Scarlet knows how to wake Natsunagi up?"

The Vampire was the person Siesta had said we'd need in order to awaken Natsunagi. Pinning our hopes on him, the two of us had set off for the Federal Council, which he'd be attending along with the other Tuners.

"It's just that there's a possibility. However, while he may not look it, he is *an expert on life and death,* so he'll have some personal views on human consciousness."

"...I...see?"

The Vampire had a technique that could resurrect the dead, although his revenants were only able to follow their most powerful instincts from their past life. He probably did have an insight into human life and death, their consciousness and souls, but...

"Can we count on a fantasy creature like a vampire?"

"Are you stupid, Kimi?"

"You're so unfair."

It had been a while since we last ran through that exchange.

"Vampires aren't the fanciful beings that folklore describes, and they didn't just spontaneously appear somewhere." Siesta took another sip of tea. "Everything happens for a reason. There has to be a cause. You mustn't shut your eyes to those things and rely on convenient words like 'impossible' or 'coincidence.'"

As she told me something vaguely familiar, her profile reminded me of the person I most wanted to meet right now.

"To begin with, vampires originated..." But just as Siesta was about to tell me about vampires, she cut herself off. "Oh, come to think of it, did you see today's astrology column? Taurus was in the lowest position."

"Geez, could you find a clumsier way to change the subject?" *And don't give me information I don't need. I'm gonna feel bummed all day now.* "Look, don't hide important stuff for no reason, all right? Just give me the information I need to know now."

"Well, it's fun to watch you flail around when you don't know anything."

"That's the worst reason ever."

## ◆ Two detectives, twelve justices

After a twelve-hour flight, Siesta and I arrived in New York. After dropping our luggage off at the hotel, we headed straight to the Federal Council venue.

"There's shuttle service and everything. They're really giving us VIP treatment," I said to Siesta. We were in the back seat of the black car that had been waiting for us as soon as we stepped out of the hotel. From the fact that Siesta had climbed in without hesitating, it would probably take us to our destination.

"They may be treating us like VIPs now, but we might not even be alive in a few hours," Siesta said. I didn't like the sound of that.

"Wasn't the Ace Detective supposed to be the star of this show?"

"Subjugating the primordial seed took far longer than it was supposed to. Besides, we also deviated from the future the Oracle foretold."

"...I see. You mean we drastically changed the route, and they may hold us responsible?"

In the sacred text, the original future that revolved around Seed had ended with Siesta losing to Hel, and Hel becoming Seed's vessel. To head that off, Siesta had appointed me and my knack for getting dragged into stuff as her assistant. Little by little, that move had changed the future.

However, the altered route was what we'd lived through last year: Siesta and Hel had taken each other out, Seed had lost both of his candidate vessels, and only Hel's main personality—Natsunagi—had survived.

Siesta had intended for me, Natsunagi, Saikawa, and Charlie to defeat Seed. I'd rejected that ending as well, though. I'd sworn to bring Siesta back to life, and now—Natsunagi had sacrificed herself to accomplish that goal, and after all our trials and tribulations, we'd ultimately managed to seal the primordial seed.

...Now that I thought about it, I really had been reckless. As Tuners, no wonder Ms. Fuubi had flipped her lid and Mia had cried. I'd destabilized the world for the sake of my own wish. I'd warped the future, and now Natsunagi was—

"You're as easy to read as ever." Siesta gave a small sigh. "It's all right. Nagisa's going to wake up." She smiled softly. "She may have fallen into a long sleep, assuming she's fulfilled her role. But you know that's not true, don't you? Nagisa Natsunagi isn't a proxy detective; nothing like it. She's not a stand-in for anyone. She's your one and only partner."

As if trying to convey the emotions in her words physically, she squeezed my hand, held it for a few moments, then released it.

"...I see. Yeah, you're right."

Natsunagi had lost her memories, forgotten how to live, and had been tormented by her lack of identity. However, she'd only just accepted her entire past, learned where to head, and finally discovered who she was. And now she was going to fall asleep forever? Even if Natsunagi was okay with that, I wasn't. I'd kill her twice, once for me and again for Hel.

"I've got one correction, though." Siesta looked puzzled. I gazed at her but turned to face forward before I spoke. "You're my partner, too."

She'd said Natsunagi was my only partner. But to me, Siesta was also—

"—I see." Like me, Siesta turned to face forward. As she spoke, we didn't look at each other. "We're almost there, Assistant."

She didn't say anything more. From the fact that she'd called me by my job title, though, our relationship was the same as it had always been.

Before long, the car slowly came to a stop. The rear doors opened, and I climbed out after Siesta.

"This is it, huh...?"

A grand, palatial building stood on the other side of an expansive garden. So this was where the Federal Council would convene. "Is it okay to have a top-secret meeting at such an eye-catching venue?"

"It's fine. Civilians never notice this place." Siesta strode toward the building.

"What, is it behind a magic barrier or something?" Three paces behind her, I stepped into the palace's spacious front hall.

"Twelve Tuners in total... Right now, I know about half of them."

As I climbed a long staircase, I counted the Tuners I'd met so far. There was Siesta, the Ace Detective; Ms. Fuubi, the Assassin; Scarlet, the Vampire; and Mia Whitlock, the Oracle. Plus Stephen Bluefield, the Inventor, the one I'd just met. Also, although I only knew of him, the Phantom Thief; he'd stolen Mia's sacred text and was now doing time deep underground somewhere.

"You've been involved with other Tuners, too," Siesta said, glancing back briefly.

"What do you mean? Is this going to be one of those *Saikawa was actually 'the Idol,' a Tuner* kind of punch lines?"

"From the fact that Yui's the only acquaintance you can think of, you obviously don't have many friends."

*Hey, mind your own business. Charlie counts, too.*

"Well, it's more that you were involved without being aware of it. You'll meet them right after this," Siesta told me, opting not to explain any further now. "More importantly, maybe I should tell you about a few of the members you should watch out for."

"Yeah, it would be nice if I could brace myself." I'd had way too many heart-attack-inducing surprises during that three-year journey, so I was grateful for the offer.

"Right. The particularly dangerous ones are the Magician and the Enforcer." We'd reached the top of the stairs and were walking down a long, red-carpeted hallway. Siesta continued her explanation. "The Magician is a witchlike old woman who almost never leaves the forest. They say she once used a certain secret art to destroy a whole village. But that power is the reason they made her a Tuner."

"So it's possible to become a defender of justice even if you've committed crimes?" They'd probably decided her secret art would be useful in protecting the world, but...

"That's a tough one... Still. From the perspective of what 'crime' means, the Enforcer has definitely killed more people than any other Tuner."

"That's pretty unsettling. The Tuners are the world's guardians, right?" As Ms. Fuubi and Scarlet had demonstrated, apparently you couldn't just call these people "heroes" and leave it at that.

"It depends on how you define 'justice.' In fact, the job assigned to the Enforcer is *the execution of criminals who can't be judged in the outside world.*"

"...So, a 'necessary evil,' huh?"

It was true that there were cases that the law couldn't settle adequately. Apparently, the Enforcer was an antihero who *cleaned up the aftermath* from the shadows.

"Right. He lurked in the shadows, carrying nothing but an enormous sickle, which he used to cut down criminals. In terms of pure combat skills, he's up there with the Assassin and even the Vampire."

"The Magician and the Enforcer, hm? I'd rather avoid getting dragged into any unnecessary... Whoops."

*Nope. If I say any more than that, I'll jinx myself.*

As I hastily clapped a hand over my mouth, we came to a set of doors that was larger than the others.

"Listen, Assistant." Siesta shot me a glance. "From this point on, don't think the common sense that has worked for you before will still apply."

Yeah. I could see that from what she'd just said and from the Tuners I'd met so far.

We exchanged nods. Then she pushed the doors open with both hands— and in the large room beyond them, we saw...

"What Rill is trying to say is—how come the Ace Detective is allowed to do whatever she wants when the rest of us can't?"

"Huh? So you're jealous of her, and you're pitching a fit because you want to get your way all the time, too?"

A girl had jumped up onto a long table. She was holding a black cane like a weapon...and glaring at Fuubi Kase. The redheaded policewoman was slouched in a chair, smoking a cigarette and gave an equally intense scowl.

The girl on the table looked quite a bit younger than the Magician, and the weapon she was holding didn't seem to be the Enforcer's sickle. In that case, this thoroughly unreasonable kid was—

"Who do you suppose she is?" Siesta looked puzzled.

*What, you don't know, either?*

Then she really wasn't the Magician or the Enforcer?

"—This is sacred ground. Lower your weapon."

Just then, a chill that made my insides feel airborne assailed me. It felt as if someone's hand was raking the pit of my stomach.

Siesta and I, and the pair who were arguing, all looked toward the owner of the voice. A middle-aged man was sitting on a dais in the depths of the room. He didn't blink at all as he spoke. "The day's leading players have arrived. Come, let the council begin."

With one last glare at Ms. Fuubi, the girl on the table returned to her chair.

"Come on, Assistant."

Aside from us, there were six heroes at the long table.

The council to determine the world's future was about to begin.

## ◆ And so the world turned

"Ace Detective Siesta. I apologize for my late arrival," Siesta said, bowing her head to the people seated at the long table. "You too, Kimi."

As prompted, I copied Siesta—Wait, we were late?

We seated ourselves in the chairs closest to us, sitting side by side.

Some of the faces in the row of Tuners were familiar, and naturally, there were others I'd never seen before. Unfortunately, even though he'd been the one we were counting on, the Vampire didn't seem to be present.

"I don't believe we've met, Ace Detective." The girl with the cane spoke politely, but her tone and her eyes were clearly hostile. She glared at Siesta, who was sitting directly across the table from her. Although her flashy outfit was very anime, her expression was cold and stern.

"You've violated the Federal Charter's rules a zillion times, you've been granted exceptions, and on top of that, you've literally come back from the dead... Just how much do you need the world to love you, anyway? Rill wishes you'd share some of that good luck with her."

The girl who called herself Rill pointed the cane in her right hand at Siesta, who didn't resist. I wasn't able to react fast enough, and my muscles tensed.

"Enough."

That said, everyone here was a seasoned veteran who'd put their life on the line to protect the world. Maybe I was too normal to keep up, but the redheaded Assassin already had her gun pointed at the girl.

"Weren't you just told to put down your weapon, Reloaded?"

"Violating the charter is a capital offense, remember? What's the problem?"

"Even if it is, you're not the one who dishes out the punishment," Ms. Fuubi snapped.

"Fuubi. Neither are you."

The man in a suit who sat at the head of the row told Ms. Fuubi to put her gun away. Apparently his words carried the most weight with this crowd; both Ms. Fuubi and Reloaded obeyed, reluctantly stowing their weapons.

I had the feeling I'd seen that man's face somewhere before. His brown hair was combed back, and his eyes were deep green. His expensive suit fit him well; he seemed to be some sort of politician... "...Oh. Are you Fritz Stewart?" I asked.

The man let his icy mask drop and smiled with his *public face*. "Once again, it's a pleasure to meet you. I'm Fritz Stewart, mayor of New York City."

I knew it. His face was the same one I'd seen on TV.

Back when Siesta and I had spent time in this country, Fritz Stewart had already been a distinguished politician. He'd won support with his mild personality and solid track record, and he was still the acting mayor of New York. "I never thought someone like you would be a Tuner."

"Yes. I've been given the role of Revolutionary."

Revolutionary... That was a Tuner position?

"I can't discuss the specifics, but *slightly tilting the world from the shadows* is the Revolutionary's mission. You might not think so, but much like children's seesaws, governments in every era are made up of balances."

For the sake of peace, the world's balance was preserved, or sometimes broken. While he wasn't a femme fatale who seduced kings and toppled nations, Fritz Stewart the Revolutionary probably didn't limit his activities to this city. From behind the scenes, he interfered with politics and economics around the world. "Global crisis" didn't always mean aliens or the denizens of parallel worlds. People who commanded nations could destroy the planet easily.

"Fritz, are you the leader of the Tuners?" I made guess based on what I'd seen so far.

"No, no. I'm only the *moderator* for this particular session." Since I didn't know anything about this council, Fritz explained for my benefit. "Perhaps you weren't informed that we Tuners are an organization under the direct control of the Mizoev Federation, either?"

"…That's right. My business partner won't tell me anything unless I ask her. And when I do, she still won't tell me." I shot Siesta a look, but as usual, she acted as if it had nothing to do with her. She'd made black tea at some point and was elegantly enjoying a cup by herself.

"It is something I'd vaguely expected, though. If some country had taken the initiative and organized the Tuners, it had to be America, Russia, China… There weren't too many other alternatives."

At present, there were six continents: Eurasia, Africa, North America, South America, Australia, and Mizoev. When the continents had fought each other over the Akashic records in World War III, no country had sustained heavy damage; I'd heard that was due to the Mizoev Federation's "Silent Rule."

"That said, the Federation Union includes several important figures from countries besides Mizoev, and that is the entity that appoints us as Tuners. Among our group, I have been charged with moderating this council," Fritz said, wrapping up his answer to my first question. He had to be used to moderating already due to his work in politics; as far as I was concerned, he was the right guy for the job.

"Still, this is your first time taking part in a Federal Council," Fritz said, focusing on me again. "Everyone here knows about you, of course, but the reverse isn't necessarily true. Before we get into the main topic, why don't we introduce ourselves?"

…He'd just said something really scary in passing. Why did all the Tuners know about me? And why were they all watching me?

"You're sure it's okay to use up time on an outsider?"

"You and the Ace Detective are today's guests of honor," Fritz responded. "Besides, if they obtain permission in advance, all Tuners are allowed to bring one assistant to the Federal Council, or send one proxy for themselves. Just as she's done." Fritz's gaze went to the chair diagonally opposite mine.

"Come to think of it, our positions are similar, huh, Olivia?"

The Oracle's messenger wasn't a flight attendant today. She was attending as her Tuner's assistant and proxy.

"Yes. Although, the Oracle is here as well." Opening her laptop, Olivia turned it to face me—and there...

"...What are you doing?" I almost said *Mia*, but clammed up to protect her privacy. Still, the girl on the screen, who was clearly Mia Whitlock, was dressed in a shrine maiden's costume...and wearing a fox mask.

"I heard it was possible to attend online. Quite modern, don't you think?" Mia said, justifying her choice. I never thought I'd see the day when shut-ins were ahead of the times.

"—I don't need this, though," she told us, removing her mask. Olivia and the other Tuners stared at her, caught off guard.

Mia had never revealed anything about her identity before, not even her face or her name. Unless she filled us in, there was no way to know what had brought on this change of heart. Even so, her eyes were glowing with a determination to be involved with the world.

"I see. So you're already acquainted with the Oracle. I suppose I should have expected no less." Fritz watched me, intrigued. "Do you know him too, then?" He let his eyes wander, skimming over the Ace Detective and the Assassin, until they came to rest on a man in a dark suit at the very end.

"................"

Even though we were inside, the man wore sunglasses, and he sat with good posture without moving a muscle. He looked almost like an exquisitely made android; he had a stern face, and he didn't say a word.

I didn't know him. But I'd been involved with *these guys* lots of times.

"The Man in Black." Fritz introduced the man by his position, not his name. "Their organization, the Men in Black, has been collectively appointed as a Tuner. They're stationed all over the world as what you might call handymen."

"...Oh, yeah, I know what you mean."

Four years ago, they'd made me smuggle that musket just before I met Siesta at ten thousand meters. After that, they'd helped us out with jobs now and then, on Siesta's instructions. After death had temporarily separated me from Siesta, I'd relied on them personally a few times.

"That's right. The Men in Black are a replacement for a piece that went missing right before the completion of an enormous puzzle. They're the lubricant that helps rusted, immobilized gears turn again. They're the gods from the machine that appear to the characters of a certain story in order to hold the plot together."

This world was riddled with inconsistencies, but people still managed to live without any cognitive dissonance. It might be thanks to a single bullet that was fired from the darkness, invisible and unremembered.

"Am I next, then?" Another individual who'd been silent until now spoke. He sat diagonally opposite Fritz: an old man with white whiskers who wore a silk hat and a smile. "My name is Bruno. My job is to provide intelligence that's useful to the rest of you as the Information Broker." Bruno's gentle smile was exactly the kind Santa Claus would have worn if he'd really existed. "It's been quite some time since we last saw each other, Ace Detective."

"It really has. It's good to see you, Bruno." Siesta bowed her head to the elderly man with unexpected reverence. Apparently they were old friends.

"He helped you out as well, Kimi, although you didn't know it," Siesta whispered in my ear.

"During those three years, you mean?"

"Yes. A third of those incidents couldn't have been resolved without his knowledge and information."

I see. So the Tuners she'd mentioned before we got here, the ones I'd been involved with unaware, had been the Men in Black and the Information Broker.

"There's no mandatory retirement age for Tuners?" I whispered to Siesta, idly curious.

"No. And, Kimi, you say some pretty rude things without even blinking."

...It was rare for Siesta to get mad at me for a good reason. She was usually much more unfair.

"Ha-ha-ha!" Bruno sounded unexpectedly entertained. He'd heard my comment loud and clear. "Oh, it doesn't bother me. No doubt you were concerned for my health." He smiled gently.

...On the other hand, somebody who was probably capable of killing people with one look glared at me. "Listen up, you damn brat." *Sure, I count as a brat to somebody your age, Ms. Fuubi*, I thought, but I didn't say it. "He's lived ten times as long as you have, and he's still performing his duties as the Information Broker. Don't you dare disrespect him."

...Ten times my age? Then Bruno was... No, but he only looked about seventy...

"It's thanks to a rather special drug. It hasn't made me quite immortal, but I will live a tad longer than the rest of you." Bruno toyed with his beard. "It's just that, since I've lived a slightly longer life, I know a few things. The Assassin and the Ace Detective always face the world's crises squarely, out on the front line, and I respect them." Bruno turned his gentle gaze on Ms. Fuubi, then Siesta.

"Let's move on, shall we?" Fritz's introductions finally shifted to the seventh Tuner. This last one was the problem kid who'd been arguing with Ms. Fuubi when we came in...

"So we finally get to talk." Switching from the stern expression she'd worn this whole time, the girl—Reloaded—smiled rather proudly, flashing white mini-fangs. Sweeping her orange hair back, she said:

"Kimihiko Kimizuka, you are in the presence of the great Magical Girl, Reloaded. How would you like to be her pet—um, familiar?"

Why are all the girls I run into such a pain in the butt?

## ◆ The scales of justice

Once the introductions were over, the positions held by the seven attending Tuners were clear. Fritz Stewart the Revolutionary, Bruno the Information Broker, the Man in Black (name unknown), Siesta the Ace Detective, Ms. Fuubi the Assassin, Mia Whitlock the Oracle. And—

"Um, excuse me? Why is Rill the only one who just got ignored?"

The girl with vivid orange hair was still calling herself by her nickname. Thumping the table, she stood up. The jolt knocked her black cane over.

"Rill's saying it one more time, Kimihiko Kimizuka: Be her familiar."

This was the seventh Tuner, Reloaded the Magical Girl. She was probably about the same age as Siesta and me, but what she was wearing looked exactly like the sort of magical girl costume you'd see in an anime. It really suited the cute expression she'd shown for a fraction of a second earlier.

However, nothing she'd said or done this whole time had been cute at all. I guessed "familiar" was a magical girl term, and she was actually telling me to be her errand boy. Meaning...

"...I really doubt there's anything in it for me."

"Oh, no, that's not true. You must be getting tired of being the Ace Detective's assistant. Being a cute magical girl's dog is bound to be more fun."

"You totally just said 'dog.' ...And anyway, why me?" I didn't even have to think about it; I knew for a fact that I was meeting this girl for the first time. Why was she trying to make me her dog...or, uh, her assistant?

"Isn't it obvious? Kimihiko Kimizuka, you are this world's—"

"—Sorry, but my assistant's never going to be yours," Siesta cut in. Reloaded had been picking a fight with her since before the council began, and Siesta finally looked ready to take her up on it. She didn't go for her weapon, but a cold war was starting across the table.

"What? You're planning to monopolize him? Nobody likes jealous women, you know."

"It's not a question of petty emotions. It's a contractual issue."

"A contract? After three or four years, they generally get renewed."

"Nice try, but no. The contract was for lifetime employment. He doesn't have time to be your partner."

...I seemed to have found myself in some sort of mystery pact with Siesta. Did "lifetime employment" mean I'd be with her until I died? That the rest of my life would be full of unfairness? ................Yeah, I should turn that down. No reason to hesitate there.

"Are you planning to *cheat*, all by yourself?" Reloaded snapped at Siesta again. "If Rill could just use the Singularity, she could do her job more efficiently..."

"Reloaded, you always manage your duties as the Magician quite well," Fritz said, attempting to defuse the situation with a compliment.

"I told you, Rill is the Magical Girl, not the Magician. She *did you the favor* of becoming a Tuner, so you said you'd change the position's name." Reloaded propped her chin in her hands, scowling at Fritz.

Apparently, Reloaded had taken over the position of Magician from the old woman Siesta had told me about on our way here. I'd just been told there was no mandatory retirement age for Tuners, so why had the previous Magician decided to step down? The mysteries and questions kept piling up, and nobody—including the prim-faced Ace Detective next to me—was providing any answers.

"—Now then. Let's begin our discussion on the main topic," Fritz said in a voice that seemed to sink into the pits of our stomachs. We were finally getting down to business. I'd heard that a report on the subjugation of the primordial seed was on the meeting's agenda, and sure enough...

"All right. We're running behind schedule, but once again, *Daydream*: Thanks to you, the crisis of the primordial seed has passed." Turning to Siesta, Fritz congratulated her on her work as the Ace Detective. "The secret society SPES should be wiped out soon, including its collaborators around the world. It has also been decided that the remote island they had illegally occupied will become a Mizoev Federation territory. The 'primordial seed' crisis has been completely resolved. Well done."

Several people applauded. Mia (on the screen), Olivia, Fritz, and Bruno all congratulated Siesta on completing her great mission.

"I..." But Siesta's face was far from cheerful.

Six years ago, she'd encountered the primordial seed. Four years ago, she'd left on a journey to battle SPES with me. If you added up all the things she'd lost along the way, she couldn't possibly put on a smile here. It wasn't the kind of girl she was.

"She didn't exactly do a praiseworthy job, though." The self-declared Magical Girl gave Siesta a cold look; her chin was still propped on her hands. "And several other Tuners broke the rules." She widened her attack to include people besides Siesta.

I'd already guessed who she was talking about.

"Fritz, you already know, don't you? The Assassin and Oracle overstepped their authority."

...I knew it. She was right: Those two had helped subjugate Seed, even though the job had been assigned to Siesta. Mia had shown Siesta the sacred text, although no one but the Oracle was allowed to view those books. After Siesta's death, Ms. Fuubi had helped Charlie and me fight SPES. Reloaded was suggesting that they'd violated the Federal Charter.

"......! It isn't Boss's fault," said the girl in the computer. "I acted of my own accord, so Boss isn't..."

"Huh? So what? You're not refuting anything, you know."

"...Olivia, how do you shut off this call screen?"

Mia wasn't used to fighting—she wasn't even used to talking to people. Shrinking under the pressure, she dejectedly tried to retreat. Pathetic, but also cute.

"Let me explain." Bruno the Information Broker raised his gloved right hand. "Truth be told, I received a proposal from the Assassin about this earlier. Certainly, the Federal Charter stipulates that one Tuner is to deal with each global crisis. However..." Bruno thumped the floor with his cane. "The Assassin asked whether it would be acceptable to assist another Tuner, provided she was *on top of* her own mission. In fact, while it is part of my duty, I myself assist other Tuners. I understood her argument quite well."

In response to Bruno's comment, all eyes turned to Ms. Fuubi.

So, knowing that her actions would cause a problem someday, Ms. Fuubi

had gone to the Information Broker about it in advance, since he was both the oldest member and the one most likely to understand what the job entailed.

"See, when a police officer notices someone in trouble, it's only natural to help them." Even with all that attention on her, Ms. Fuubi stayed cool and composed enough to crack jokes. Not only that, but... "Well, that might be too much to process for a little kid who's struggling so much with her own mission that she can't afford to be considerate of other people." She snorted, clearly mocking a certain someone.

"Are you talking about Rill?"

"Oh, so you knew you were like that?"

"Huhn?"

"Uhn?"

...Ms. Fuubi, you suck at interacting with people.

"I see. I understand the situation." For now, with no change in his expression, Fritz accepted Ms. Fuubi and Bruno's claims. "It's true that the threat from the primordial seed was on a level not often seen in recent years. We should be able to allow a few irregularities."

"—You're just a mediator. You don't have the authority to make that decision." Unable to accept the decision, Reloaded snapped at Fritz.

"Correct. If it comes down to officially changing the rules, the Federation Government will make the ultimate decision. That said..." Fritz's tone changed again. "I handed down that judgment on the understanding that, right now, our top priority should be the smooth progression of this meeting. Are there any objections?"

He spoke in a voice that chilled me to the bone, and I felt a phantom pain run through my heart. Even though she'd acted so arrogant, Reloaded flinched, then backed down.

"That appears to be settled, then." Bruno's hoarse voice broke the silence; he'd chosen to ignore the tension. "A new age calls for new rules and values. I am proud of young people who don't fear such changes. ...Or perhaps this senile old codger is simply desperate to keep up with the times." He gently stroked his cane with his fingertips.

"Thank you for your consideration." Ms. Fuubi bowed her head to the Information Broker. Like Siesta, she seemed to have a genuine respect for Bruno.

"Ha-ha-ha. It was a request from a cute girl, after all."

"...Thank you for your consideration." After a brief pause, Ms. Fuubi responded with the exact same line she'd said before. Uncharacteristically, she didn't seem to know how to react, and a laugh escaped me—almost. Man, that was close.

"All right, *shall we discuss the main topic?*"

—Fritz's cold eyes turned toward me.

*Oh, I get it.* That was when it hit me: The council's objective wasn't to hear a simple report about the primordial seed's subjugation. This was...

"The future written in the sacred text has changed. What are your views on that?"

Its goal was to denounce me for messing with the future Mia had prophesied and searched for the brand-new Route X.

"I heard Daydream should have died. The next Ace Detective would have been the one to defeat the primordial seed. You rejected that and twisted the narrative—and as a result, Daydream returned to life. However, we lost Nagisa Natsunagi, the next candidate for Ace Detective. At least, I'm told she's currently comatose." Fritz looked at me, one eyebrow raised. "Was this truly what you... No, what Daydream wanted?" Fritz was asking me and only me. This was an interrogation. Did I think Siesta had wanted to trade Natsunagi's life for her own? I couldn't reply. I was all too aware of the answer.

"The Singularity."

As Fritz said that word, he looked at me, and the eyes of the other Tuners all focused on me as well.

"When an era begins to experience dramatic changes, *it* inevitably appears. It overturns the future the Oracle foretells, transforming the world's set path. An irregular element—that's you," Fritz stated.

The Singularity. A while back, Scarlet had mentioned that word once. I also got the feeling Mia had said something similar, and that she'd been watching me when she said it.

An irregular entity capable of changing the future, of setting the world in motion... That was me, Kimihiko Kimizuka. *That's not even funny. There's no way something that ridiculous could be true.* Internally, I laughed the idea off, but signs of subtle foreshadowing in my past flickered through my mind.

There was my irritating tendency to get dragged into things. Could that actually be because I was the Singularity, and my nature kept setting off unexpected trouble around me? Come to think of it, Hel had once told me that my predisposition was the type that transformed things and triggered incidents, and that I was the center of the world. Not to mention how a certain ace detective had taken me ten thousand meters into the sky because she'd needed me to help her change a disastrous future.

What if I assumed that all those things had been because I was this "Singularity"? That was why incidents happened around me, why I attracted detectives and enemies of the world, and had even overturned the Oracle's prophesied future. The real reason I'd managed to pull off a taboo like resurrecting the dead was—

"Let me ask you this, Singularity. How will you involve yourself with the world from now on?" Fritz asked me. "It's true that this time, partly due to the cooperation of other Tuners, Daydream returned to life as you had planned. The elimination of the primordial seed also *happened* to go well, but that won't always be the case. To me, results aren't everything."

I was silent. Keeping his eyes on me, Fritz Stewart laced his fingers together, resting his elbows on the table. Ms. Fuubi and Mia couldn't argue, either. Even if they didn't come out and say what they'd done was wrong, they had to know it hadn't been right.

I knew that better than anyone, though. I'd made Ms. Fuubi mad, I'd made Mia cry, but I'd still convinced both of them. I'd deceived them. In that case, I'd have to be the one to say it.

"Assistant?"

I'd abruptly stood up, and Siesta stared at me, startled.

Until now, I'd relied exclusively on the detective. For those three years, I'd been with Siesta all the time. I'd been too quick to rely on her, to believe that as long as she was there, the cases would be solved and our wishes would come true. ...And I'd paid for that when I lost her. Unable to forget her, I'd spent a whole year doing nothing, and then I'd met a new detective.

It was fine for Natsunagi to live her own life. I'd told her so myself, and yet in the end, I'd asked her to continue being a detective. Once again, I'd come to rely on her completely. During those three years, and that year of tepid idleness, and these past few months when I'd gotten back on my feet, I'd constantly clung to and been saved by a detective. But...

"It's probably about time we switched places, huh?"

That had to be why I was standing here today.

My legs had been weirdly shaky for the past few minutes, but hey, I wasn't going to worry about it. It was just fatigue from sitting for a long time without shifting positions—No, I was quivering from the adrenaline.

"Fritz. You're saying it's a problem that we tried to bring Siesta back to life, right?" I looked at the Revolutionary, then let my gaze travel across the other attendees. I was a regular guy, surrounded by Tuners; technically, it was presumptuous of me even to speak here. What on earth could I say, with the eyes of all these global heroes on me?

"Simply put, yes, that is what I'm saying," Fritz answered for the group, without turning a hair. He spoke, not with his public politician's face, but as the Revolutionary who pulled the strings of the underworld. "In the original route, the Ace Detective would have been sacrificed to save the world."

This representative of the world's guardians had determined that the detective should have died.

When I heard that, my mind grew oddly calm. The Tuners' rules, the story recorded in the sacred text, whether or not I was the Singularity—none of that had anything to do with this. There was only one thing that really mattered. I already knew what I had to say.

"I see. So Siesta shouldn't have come back to life, huh? Do you seriously think that? If so, *you people should quit this job right now.*"

I mean, if they couldn't understand something so simple...

People like that weren't qualified to protect the world, were they?

"Losing Siesta is a loss for all of humanity, the whole world, the entire universe."

Ever since the day when I'd met the detective at ten thousand meters, she—no, both of them—had held out their hands to me. All this time, they'd saved me. From now on, though, it would be the other way around. It didn't matter whether I was the Singularity. I didn't care about the world. The only thing I couldn't give up was...

Siesta. Natsunagi.

I wasn't letting the detectives die.

"..............."

Silence fell. In the stillness, all I could hear was my own heartbeat. Of the seven Tuners, some glared at me, others wore intrigued smiles or gazed indifferently into space. After the seemingly endless silence had stretched on for thirty seconds or so...

"...Well, that's what I think, but let's leave the actual decision to the higher-ups."

"Are you stupid, Kimi?"

Unable to take the silence any longer, I returned dejectedly to my seat. As expected, Siesta gave me a cold, clammy look. Before long, she heaved a big sigh.

"Still—thank you."

She seemed vaguely troubled, but she had on a faint smile. "I suppose I can't make my assistant work that hard and then say nothing myself." As if taking my place, Siesta rose to her feet. "Naturally, I'm prepared to take responsibility for this incident."

Scanning every face in the room, she spoke calmly.

★　★　★

"I hereby declare my resignation as a Tuner. I would like to officially nominate Nagisa Natsunagi as the next Ace Detective."

## ◆ The detective, beaten hollow

After the Federal Council, Siesta and I went to a trendy cafeteria near our hotel for a light dinner. We got ourselves some pasta and scones and other things, and then we planned for the fallout of that council.

"What's this about, Siesta?" I asked. She was twisting up neat forkfuls of pasta. "Are you seriously stepping down as Ace Detective?"

At the Federal Council about an hour ago, Siesta had declared that she was leaving the position of Ace Detective, and had nominated Natsunagi to replace her. However, the other Tuners (except for Mia) had seemed perfectly unruffled by her announcement.

"Oh, that? I just assumed you were going to ask about the Singularity." As primly as ever, Siesta dabbed at her lips with a napkin.

"If I said I wasn't curious, I'd be lying...but there's something else I need to prioritize now."

"I see. I thought you'd yell at me for not telling you about important things like that beforehand." From the way she was talking, Siesta had been aware that I was *that sort of thing*. At least for now, though, that information was relatively unimportant to me. "Let's say I really do have some sort of effect on the world. *That won't influence what I do.*"

I'd had this insanely troublesome knack for getting dragged into stuff my whole life. At this point, giving it a different definition wasn't going to change anything about how I thought or lived. There was just one thing I needed to do, one wish I want granted.

"...I see. Heh-heh. You really have grown, Kimi." Seeming to have convinced herself of something, Siesta resumed her meal.

"And? I'm asking why you suddenly said you were quitting as the Ace Detective."

She'd wrapped things up in a vague sort of way with a good story, but Siesta had a particular talent for glossing over the important details.

"My mission as Ace Detective was to annihilate SPES, nothing more. Now that I've done that, I don't think it's odd for me to resign from the position."

"...Didn't you tell me you were born to be a detective?" As I asked her that, I was studying the glass near my hand. I could see my own warped reflection in the water.

"That's right. And so, now that I've defeated my mortal enemy, I'll *go back to being an ordinary detective*. That's all." Watching me, Siesta smiled. "From now on, this is your story." Her manner was mild, but the way she spoke left me no room to argue.

"I see..." She was right, though. Even if Siesta stopped fighting the enemies of the world, she'd still be tackling the mysteries and evils that lurked in everyday life. She might have quit being the Ace Detective, but that didn't mean she'd completely vanish from my life—

"Assistant?" Immediately, I realized Siesta was peering at my face.

"...No, it's nothing." I'd decided to quit relying on the detectives for everything, and yet here I was, taking it for granted that Siesta would be with me. It surprised me, and I cleared my throat before I continued. "So you're appointing Natsunagi to take over?"

"Right. It's all thanks to Nagisa that I'm able to move like this, and that we managed to defeat Seed. I'm sure she'll be a better Ace Detective than me... No, Nagisa was better suited to it all along. She's beaten me hollow." Siesta leaned against her chair. It was as if she was admitting defeat to the Alicia version of Natsunagi we'd met in London a year ago. "Of course, that's assuming she still wants to be the Ace Detective. She may have lost the power of that seed and gone back to being an ordinary girl."

"...Yeah. We'll just have to ask her about that."

We exchanged nods, then went over our game plan. No matter how much Siesta wanted Natsunagi to take over as Ace Detective, it wasn't going to happen unless Natsunagi woke up.

"That's true. We don't have much time, but we'll wake Nagisa up for sure."

At the Federal Council, we had been told that Siesta's intention to resign would be officially communicated to the *higher-ups* on the condition that we summoned Nagisa Natsunagi to the council. In other words, unless Natsunagi woke up and agreed to inherit Siesta's will, Siesta would stay the Ace Detective.

"We didn't get to see Scarlet, though."

Siesta had planned to get a hint about how to wake Natsunagi up from the vampire, but unfortunately, he'd never showed.

"It might still have been too early. He should be fine indoors, but…"

The vampire only came out at night. Like Seed, he didn't get along with the sun. "Still, only seven Tuners attended."

The ones who hadn't come were the Vampire, the Inventor, the Phantom Thief (whom I still hadn't seen), and two more… Oh, one of those would have to be the Enforcer that Siesta had mentioned, huh?

"It's actually unusual for more than half to turn up. We were lucky we got to see the new Tuner, the Magical Girl," Siesta murmured, relieving her dry throat with a sip of tea. Saying this after the other girl had ripped her a new one—talk about imperturbable.

"She said she'd taken over for the Magician? Do positions really switch out that easily?" Although in this case, she might just have changed the name of the role.

"Oh, yes. It happens a lot. There have been more than twelve Tuner positions before, and they're tailored to their particular eras. I seem to recall that there were Exorcist and Master Swordsman positions once, long ago."

"So there's a lot of turnover."

"That's what happens when you fight the enemies of the world," Siesta said with a sad smile.

I'd only been talking about the fact that the positions changed, but Siesta had probably taken it another way. There were new Tuners on a regular basis because they were killed in the line of duty.

"As a matter of fact, it sounds as if the Enforcer I knew also disappeared during the past year."

...I see. So it wasn't just that he'd skipped the council. Does that mean another person had already taken over the Enforcer role, or had the whole position been switched out for another one?

For those three years, while Siesta had fought the enemies of the world, she'd known what was going to happen to her someday. I'd been right next to her the whole time, and I'd never picked up on her resolution.

"More importantly, we need to think about Nagisa right now." As always, Siesta got the conversation back on topic as if she'd read my mind. "I mentioned it earlier, but I think her consciousness has fallen into a deep sleep." Putting a fingertip to her chin, she began considering Natsunagi's current condition. "She thinks she's fulfilled her role. Once she came to terms with that, she felt relieved and fell asleep. That's what I did, too," she said; she was speaking from experience.

Siesta had also left her mind to live on in Natsunagi's heart and gone to sleep.

"...Hm? Then how did you do it that one time?"

"What one time?" Siesta tilted her head slightly.

"You know, on that luxury cruise ship. When I was fighting Chameleon after he lost control, you borrowed Natsunagi's body and came to help me, remember?"

At the very least, Siesta had awakened and came running to me then.

"...Did that happen?"

"Look, there's no way you can play dumb about it."

But for some reason, Siesta averted her eyes, apparently puzzled.

"Oh, I see." Just then, a certain possibility occurred to me. After being her assistant for so many years, I'd picked up some deductive skills, too. "You mean since I was in deep trouble, you panicked and woke up because you couldn't bear to just stand by and do nothing."

"......"

"On an unconscious level, you were worried sick about me."

"............"

Siesta was doing her best to hang on to her composure, but even so, her eyebrows twitched.

When I remembered the way she'd rushed to the scene in a mecha when I'd been kidnapped, that actually didn't strike me as out of character. In other words—

"Siesta, you like me that much, huh?"

A whole year later, I'd been given the opportunity to get her back.

"............Are you stupid, Kimi?"

I was rewarded with the weakest put-down I'd ever heard from her.

"......Haaah." Siesta heaved a long sigh. "Should you really be having conversations like this with me, Kimi? If Nagisa heard you, I think she'd be very angry." She stared at me, looking rather disgusted.

Now that I'd reunited with my partner after a year apart, she seemed to be more expressive than before. It was probably because she'd spent that year in constant contact with a girl who always held strong emotions. On that thought, I told her, "Yeah, I bet she would be."

—That's why.

"That's why I want her to wake up and scold me already."

That was my only wish right now.

"...Kimi, I suspect you like Nagisa far too much." Siesta smirked.

I had no idea how to respond to that prompt retort, and as I was racking my brain...

"—Nobody move!"

A man's voice and a gunshot suddenly echoed throughout the café. Wondering what happened, I turned to look and saw several masked men pointing their guns at staff members and customers.

Apparently, we had yet another *incident* on our hands. Geez. Talk about destroying the mood. Biting back a wry smile, I waited for the detective's instructions.

"Assistant. Seriously, could you do something about that predisposition of yours?"

"Yeah. That's actually the second-biggest wish I've got right now."

## ◆ The enemy's name is Arsene

The next day.

Having received a summons from a certain individual, Siesta and I were visiting the New York City Police.

"Hey, did you enjoy yourselves last night?"

We were shown into a reception room where a female police officer sat on a sofa as if she owned it, a cigarette in one hand. With a line that reminded me of a certain famous RPG, Fuubi Kase smirked at Siesta and me.

"I don't get what you mean by 'enjoy ourselves.'" Playing dumb, I sat down on the sofa across from Ms. Fuubi, next to Siesta.

"Oh, you know. The young lady over there looks sleepy. I thought maybe you'd kept her up all night."

"...This ace detective always looks sleepy." I glanced over at Siesta. She was rubbing her eyes; it wasn't clear whether she was listening to me and Ms. Fuubi. Now that I thought about it, she did seem to be having a harder time waking up than usual...but I swear to God we hadn't done anything last night. Not that I should even have to point that out.

"Actually, Ms. Fuubi, why are you so comfortable at the NYPD?"

A rank-and-file Japanese police officer had occupied this room as if she was the boss and was puffing away on a cigarette. And I thought she'd said she'd quit smoking.

"Oh, this? I'd love to kick the habit right this minute, but..." Ms. Fuubi smiled thinly. "I figured I'd smoke enough for that guy too for a while."

I hadn't expected that. In her own way, she was paying her tribute to her deceased enemy.

"...And? You wanted to talk about yesterday's incident?" I meant the masked mystery men who'd attacked the café where we'd had dinner the night before. Unfortunately for them, one of the diners had been the Ace Detective. In the end, Siesta subdued them before I could even attempt to do something cool, and we'd handed them over to the police.

Since we'd at least partially completed our objectives, we'd been thinking about heading back to Japan today. Right before we did, though, Ms. Fuubi had contacted us about the incident, and so here we were.

"Yeah. We got the crew you hauled in yesterday to cough up their motive for that attack. And, y'know, they said something kinda interesting."

Anything Ms. Fuubi said was "interesting" was definitely going to be a pain in the butt for us. Drooping in resignation, I listened to what she had to say—

"They said, 'Free Arsene.'"

The moment Siesta heard that, she flinched. So much for the sleepiness from earlier. Then she put a fingertip to her chin, looking grim. I didn't yet know why, though. Arsene? Who was that?

"He's the Phantom Thief."

"…! The Phantom Thief? You can't mean…"

Siesta nodded. "That's right. One of the twelve Tuners—the traitor, Phantom Thief Arsene. Although I'm told that isn't his real name," she added. She seemed conflicted.

*The traitorous* Phantom Thief Arsene. The Oracle, Mia Whitlock, had explained the reasons behind that modifier to us earlier.

The Phantom Thief had made some sort of deal with Seed and stolen the sacred text from Mia. Tuners were supposed to be allies of justice, of course, and this had been a blatant breach of faith. As a result, he'd been confined in an underground prison.

"They tell me there've been frequent acts of terror here in New York lately, with the goal of setting him free. That Fritz louse is hard-pressed to deal with them all." Exhaling a puff of smoke, Ms. Fuubi brought up the name of the Revolutionary, who worked as a politician.

"It isn't just New York, either. We're getting scattered reports of similar occurrences from around the world. What do you think? Ring any bells?" Ms. Fuubi's sharp eyes turned to me.

"Don't tell me… Was that busjacking in London part of this?" It had happened about three weeks ago, when I was taking a bus through London with Mia. I was pretty sure the man with a gun had demanded that the police "free his comrade." By "comrade," he'd meant Phantom Thief Arsene?

"Does the Phantom Thief have that many friends?" Companions who'd hijack buses or barricade themselves into buildings in New York, London, and all around the world in attempts to rescue him...

"I had heard he had a lot of *collaborators*," Siesta responded. "But I doubt..."

"Yeah, the people working to get him released definitely aren't his friends." Ms. Fuubi finished Siesta's thought for her. "They didn't know anything specific about the Phantom Thief other than his false name, Arsene."

Ms. Fuubi seemed sure about that, so the men probably weren't lying to protect the Phantom Thief. If so... "You're saying they were just disposable pawns of his?"

"That, or..." Ms. Fuubi stubbed out her cigarette in an ashtray, cutting me off. "Arsene may be *controlling them however he wants.*"

Ordering people around the world, individuals he'd never seen, to break him out of prison.

"...Is that even possible?" Did Arsene have a technique that let him use complete strangers like puppets?

"I don't know how he does it specifically. But..." Siesta's expression was unusually grim. "He is the Phantom Thief: *He can steal anything, even human hearts and wills.*"

"...! But if Arsene is plotting to break out of jail, can't we stop it somehow?"

I'd been told he was locked up deep underground in some unknown country. In that case, if we took proper steps before he made any further moves—

"Yeah. *It would have been great if we'd done that, but...*" Ms. Fuubi answered in Siesta's place, blowing smoke toward the ceiling. "According to the incompetent higher-ups, Phantom Thief Arsene has already escaped."

### ◆ The buzzer's sure to sound three times

After leaving the police station, we discussed Phantom Thief Arsene... Or that's what I figured we'd do, but Siesta betrayed my expectations.

"These two should be ours."

Siesta and I lowered ourselves into a pair of theater seats. For some reason, we were at a Broadway theater to catch a musical.

"Now really isn't the time for stuff like this."

"Hurrying won't necessarily help us find the answer we're looking for," Siesta declared calmly, looking down at the pamphlet in her hands. There had to be some kind of logic behind this decision of hers, right? "Still, it's been a long time since we did this. Two years ago, wasn't it?" she asked, reminiscing. We'd visited this theater before, on her suggestion. "Last time, there was a terrorist incident during the show, so we weren't able to enjoy it properly."

"So this is a redo, huh? ...Actually, it seems like all we do is get dragged into stuff like that."

"Mostly because of you, Kimi."

We spent the time before the curtain went up bantering.

It had been two years.

Back then, I seemed to remember talking about making it up later. However, a year after that, I'd realized that was a promise we wouldn't get to keep. Who'd have thought it would happen now...?

"Well? Over the past year, have you matured into a man who looks good at musicals and other stylish cultural scenes?"

"Well, I am eighteen and all. Formal situations don't make me nervous, and escorting women is my specialty," I told her, dodging her probing question. "During the past year, not only have I gone shopping with them and had dinner with them, but I've hung out with them at pools and casinos while on vacation. I can even invite them to bars."

"...I see. Not that it has anything to do with me if you grow up and get along well with other women."

I'd managed to step on some sort of landmine. Siesta's mood had obviously soured.

"I'm kidding. All those women were either Natsunagi, Saikawa, or Charlie."

Not only that, but it had all happened over the past couple of months.

From Siesta's death until I met Natsunagi, I'd done nothing but soak in tepid routine.

"It is true that I've gained more experience with a lot of stuff, though," I told her. Siesta looked at me, perplexed. "Well, you know. First, let's wake up Natsunagi. After that, once things calm down—"

As we talked, we were dreaming of a day somewhere in the future.

"Want to go somewhere together?"

"—Yes, that sounds good."

The opening buzzer sounded.

"There's nothing like a Broadway musical on actual Broadway, is there?"

Three hours later, as we walked back to our hotel, Siesta stretched. Her hands reached up toward the sky and the crescent moon far overhead.

"The funniest part was when the two leads started making out and you got really uncomfortable."

"Don't enjoy it in ways that make no sense. Watch the show, not me."

"Oh, then I guessed right? It was so dark, I couldn't actually see your face."

That was a dirty trick...

The corners of Siesta's lips curved up slightly. Then she took three steps ahead of me. "We should be getting back to Japan, though."

"...Yeah, I'm worried about Natsunagi."

In the end, we hadn't managed to see Scarlet and currently had no clues on how to wake Natsunagi. There was no point in staying here any longer. As Siesta said, we should return to Japan as soon as possible.

"........."

"Assistant?" The next thing I knew, Siesta was standing in front of me, looking into my face. "Were you thinking about the Phantom Thief?"

...This ace detective really did see everything. What Ms. Fuubi had told us was still bothering me. "Yeah. I was wondering how a jailbird turned people around the world into terrorists."

Even if Phantom Thief Arsène did have a way to control others like Ms. Fuubi and Siesta said, it seemed like it would be tough to pull off from inside a cell.

"Good point. If he'd manipulated a prison guard, for example, it would have been easy for him to break out himself. I can't think of a reason for him to do that to total strangers all over the world."

Exactly. The tactic Arsene had used seemed like an extremely round-about way of doing things. If breaking out of prison had been his first and only goal, there had to have been a more efficient method. There was a major contradiction between what Arsene was capable of and the results of his actions. That seemed to be the biggest mystery here.

"Do you know anything else about the Phantom Thief, Siesta?" Up until now, she'd never gone out of her way to tell me things. However, since I'd learned about the Tuners and gotten closer to the world's darker side, she probably wouldn't hide information without a good reason now.

"Arsene always was a mysterious figure. Even I don't know much about him, besides his abilities as a phantom thief. However, one thing I do know is that..."

With that preface, Siesta gave me new information on the Phantom Thief.

*"If Arsene steals from someone, that person will never notice."*

According to Siesta, he'd been given the position of Phantom Thief in recognition of those overwhelming skills.

The victim would never realize something went missing, much less that it had been stolen. The old me would probably have wondered if that was possible; I wouldn't have been convinced. However, I'd forgotten the truth of Siesta's death once, because of that pollen. Siesta had also had her memories of meeting Natsunagi and Alicia stolen.

Things that were lost this way were washed out to sea and over the horizon by fuzzy, pixelated waves, without their owner ever noticing they'd vanished. Could Phantom Thief Arsene steal wills and hearts that deftly, too? And his victims would never even know he'd done it...

"Still." As I stood silent, Siesta continued. "You're actively trying to solve this incident. Even though you used to look so put out whenever I brought in a job... You've grown." Stretching a little, Siesta patted my head. "Physically too, at some point." For some reason, her smile looked lonely.

"...Quit it." I reached up to knock her hand away, but my regrets raced through my mind, and I ended up lowering my arm again.

As Siesta said, we didn't necessarily have to be the ones to solve this problem. Ms. Fuubi might have gone out of her way to bring it up to us because she was hoping for something from the Ace Detective, but even then, no one was forcing us. Still, I'd stuck my nose into this case because—

"If I seem enthusiastic, it's because this job is special."

"Special?" Siesta tousled my hair, looking perplexed.

*...If I don't make her stop soon, my hair will be too messy to be seen in public at all.*

"Yeah. According to what Mia told me, the Phantom Thief asked Seed for something as a condition for stealing the sacred text. If what he asked for was one of his seeds, I thought it might be the key to solving this case."

In other words, I'd thought this might be an *extra inning* of the primordial seed crisis. If so, then the Ace Detective and her assistant should deal with this as well.

"—I see." Seeming satisfied, Siesta removed her hand from my head.

"Even so, wasn't there anything they could have done before he escaped?" Why should we have to scramble like this now? I grumbled about the other Tuners and the group above them. "And they didn't strip the position of Phantom Thief from Arsene? Why not? If he stole the sacred text, it wouldn't have been a crazy thing to do."

"I don't know much about what's happened during the past year, but the selection of Tuners is ultimately the decision of the top brass. They may have had a reason to let Arsene stay the Phantom Thief and to lock him up instead of killing him. Apart from whether or not that was the right move..." Siesta wrapped up her speech.

"But, yes." She gave me two light pats on the shoulder. "You're able to view things from multiple angles now. Continue to develop that trait."

"...I haven't heard that irritating compliment in quite a while."

"And so..." Siesta fixed her straightforward blue eyes on me. "I want you to stay by Nagisa's side and support her." As she said it, she took her left hand from my shoulder. Just as I was about to respond—"Assistant, it looks like it's about time."

"Time? ...!"

The alley was dark; the sun had gone down completely.

As if seeping out of the darkness, or from the shadows of the electric lights, the white demon appeared.

One of the twelve shields that protected the world—the Vampire, Scarlet.

His glaring golden eyes were fixed on the person next to me, as if he were sizing up his prey. When he spoke, I saw red blood on his teeth.

"It's been a long time—Daydream."

## ◆ The white demon and the whereabouts of the soul

His white suit seemed to float in the darkness, and his red necktie reminded me of blood.

This man's name was Scarlet—and he was an actual *vampire*.

I'd first encountered him a few weeks ago, in the parking garage under a TV station. Ever since then, it had been really hard to say whether we were enemies or allies.

"We finally meet," Siesta said. Smiling a little, she gazed at the vampire who was leaning against the wall.

Apparently she'd *adjusted our schedule* so that we'd meet him here. The vampire never appeared outside while the sun was up. Siesta hadn't gone to that musical just for fun.

"Ha! I see, I see. You missed me so much that you returned from the dead, hm? What an admirable woman." Scarlet nodded to himself with apparent satisfaction.

"Um, no. I came to see you because I just happened to have business with you, that's all."

"There's no need to be embarrassed. Not as my former bride candidate."

"Scarlet, what did you just say? 'Bride'? Siesta is? Whose?"

"Assistant, don't make the conversation more complicated. And don't draw your gun over a thing like this."

...She could say that, but from the way Scarlet had talked before, there was definitely some sort of deep history between these two. There was a decent possibility that he had something on Siesta and was threatening her, for example. If so, as her assistant, wasn't there, you know, something I should do?

"And we've met again sooner than I expected, human." As I was thinking, Scarlet's eyes had turned to me.

"...Yeah. We came to pick your brain about something." I had plenty of other things to discuss with this guy right now besides his relationship with Siesta. The ace detective and I exchanged looks, then got down to business.

"Scarlet." Siesta took half a step toward the vampire. "Do you know how to return consciousness to a human who won't wake up?"

That was why she'd come to consult the Vampire after the Inventor.

As a vampire, Scarlet could raise the dead. Those he revived came back empty of everything except the strongest instinct they'd developed while they were alive. In other words, we thought he might be able to draw human instincts or awareness to the surface. Siesta was asking Scarlet how to wake up our sleeping friend.

"Where do you suppose human souls dwell?" Scarlet asked us instead of answering. "In the brain, or *there*?" His golden eyes looked down at the left side of Siesta's chest.

Where in the body was the human "heart," or soul, located? Even if I got a little more specific and replaced those terms with "consciousness"—even then, philosophy, psychology, medicine, and the other sciences would each give different answers. Philosophy put more weight on thought. Psychology emphasized sensation. Medicine made distinctions based on stimulus and response. There were infinite ways to interpret human consciousness.

In Siesta's case, possibly due to the effects of the seed, her consciousness had been in her physical heart. Meanwhile, since Hel was Natsunagi's second personality, she'd probably slept in her mind, as a backup of sorts.

Since Natsunagi was the main personality, was her awareness also generated by her brain? In scientific terms, that might be the case.

"........"

I realized that Scarlet was gazing at me, a faint, cold smile on his face. "The whereabouts of human consciousness... Well, I don't know the answer to that myself." He looked as if he were showing off.

*What, you act all mysterious, and then you don't know, either?*

"That was the world's biggest waste of time..."

"And he acts so proud of it." Siesta gave Scarlet a disgusted look.

"There's no help for that. The Undead I create *arbitrarily* come back with an instinct intact. My will has nothing to do with it."

"You mean it doesn't happen because you want it to?"

"No, just as I'm not living like this because I want to." Scarlet's response was inscrutable. I wanted to ask what he meant, but his beautiful, terrible profile gave me pause.

"The one thing I can say is this," he told us. "Even if it's only a strand of their hair or a bit of a tooth, as long as I have a physical piece of them, the dead will come back. In that sense, human instinct, or consciousness, must dwell in every fragment of their DNA." By the time Scarlet finished that sentence, he'd resumed his usual aloof expression.

Human consciousness ran through the entire body, from the tips of our toes to the crowns of our heads, circulating like blood. It was as if an inexhaustible will lived in the eyes that existed to see tomorrow, in the hands that took up a sword to protect someone, in the heart that didn't stop beating even after death.

"Bat's dead."

Then, I'd remembered one of our mortal enemies, and I told Scarlet about him.

Scarlet had been with Bat on the night I met him; he'd said their interests had aligned. One thing led to another, and Bat had eventually sided with me and Saikawa instead of Scarlet. Achieving a long-cherished ambition, he'd finally fought Seed and had fallen in battle.

"I see," Scarlet murmured. He didn't seem to feel anything in particular about the news. "If you bring me *a piece* of him, I can revive him."

He probably wasn't trying to be a jerk. As a vampire, he was just making the suggestion as a matter of course.

"No, it's fine." I didn't even have to speak for the dead. I knew full well Bat would never want that. After all... "He already got his wish."

He didn't need to fight anymore. I wanted him to rest in peace.

"I see. I don't understand it myself, but no doubt that's a good thing." Scarlet gazed into the distance. The night wind toyed with his silver hair.

"There's one other thing I want to ask you," Siesta said. "Do you know what sort of deal Arsène struck with Seed long ago?"

That was the second issue we had on our hands right now: What had Arsène gotten from Seed in exchange for the sacred text? That might be the hint to solving the mystery behind this chain of incidents.

"Who knows? I haven't been to that wearisome council in ages, so I know nothing about that sort of thing." Scarlet shrugged, refusing to give us the answer we were looking for again. "Besides, the only things that interest me are my enemies."

Did he mean the world's enemies, as a Tuner? Or—

"Scarlet, what are you fighting against?"

The vampire didn't answer. His golden eyes gazed at the faraway moon as if it dazzled him.

"Ah, but there was one thing I needed to tell you." Remembering something, Scarlet turned to look at us again. "While I have no way of knowing about the Phantom Thief, I can provide information about the deceased primordial seed. As a reward for defeating him, you see." His smile was as arrogant as ever. "When I negotiated with Seed, he asked if I would help him extinguish the sun."

That had probably been what Scarlet had mentioned earlier, the "united front" Seed had proposed. I'd asked him what sort of negotiations they'd had before, but he'd evaded the question that time, pretending not to hear.

"So that's what it was, huh?" Frankly, when we'd learned that Seed's weakness was the sun, I'd had an idea that that might have been it. Scarlet was just as bad with sunlight as Seed was; that was why Seed had negotiated with him.

"Why did you turn him down, though? That was a pretty good offer for a vampire, wasn't it?"

"Yes. It was an entertaining suggestion, and I thought it would be amusing to go along with him. However..." Scarlet's gaze shifted from me to Siesta. "It would have meant my former bride candidate could no longer nap in the sunlight, and I took pity on her." His expression softened.

"...Well. If we're comparing the number of times we've seen Siesta's sleeping face, then I've—"

"Assistant, I don't see the point of competing with him on that."

I wasn't competing. I was just stating facts.

Still, at this point we'd asked Scarlet everything we needed to. We probably wouldn't make any more progress regarding Natsunagi's consciousness or the Phantom Thief. On that thought, I signaled to Siesta that we should probably be going.

"There's no telling what the Phantom Thief may do. You be careful as well," Siesta told Scarlet as we turned to leave.

"You're very considerate toward your husband," the guy murmured, sounding satisfied.

*Who's "Siesta's husband," huh? I'll kick your ass.*

"But it's true that there has been suspicious movement lately." Scarlet's golden eyes narrowed. "About a month ago, I received the corpse of a certain man. The sender asked *if I would purchase it for a million dollars.*"

It sounded almost like the organ trade—although the act of buying and selling human corpses was probably significant to a vampire who could raise the dead.

"So the corpse didn't belong to an ordinary human?" I asked, picking up on the direction of the conversation.

"Correct. I did not purchase it, but no doubt it was a fair price for the individual."

Then Scarlet told us about the dead man he'd seen a month ago.

"It was the corpse of Fritz Stewart, the Revolutionary."

## ◆ The curtain rises on the next story

The next day, Siesta and I were in a room of a certain building.

It was past four in the afternoon.

We sat side by side on a sofa meant for visitors, waiting for *the person we were meeting* to arrive.

"Your deduction skills have improved," Siesta told me. She'd put the tea set she'd brought with her to work and was enjoying a cup of tea.

After parting with Scarlet the night before, I'd put together a hypothesis about the chain of incidents centered around the Phantom Thief, and once we returned to the hotel, I'd spent the entire night discussing it with Siesta. Having reached a certain conclusion, we'd come to visit this person in order to confirm our answers.

"I could sense that you'd grown last night as we walked down the street. Who'd have guessed you were the type who'd evolve even further in combat?" Siesta was talking as if I were the hero of an action manga. "You've grown up while I wasn't looking. The days when I changed your diapers are just a fond memory now."

"That definitely never happened. If anyone's a baby here, it's you. Just how late do you think you slept in today anyway?"

In a repeat of yesterday, Siesta hadn't woken this morning and slept until noon. In the evening, after I'd shaken her over and over, she'd finally crawled out of bed.

"It's all right once in a while, isn't it?" Siesta primly shrugged off my sarcasm.

*I'm saying it's a problem because it's not "once in a while," okay?*

"Besides, *the other party* is also busy. This was the only time available."

"Well, we did get here by the appointed time, but still…"

In the middle of our conversation, the door abruptly opened, and someone walked in. He hadn't knocked. That was only natural: He was *the owner of this office.*

"Did I keep you waiting?"

The man's name was Fritz Stewart.

He was wearing an expensive suit and a business smile. Instead of sitting down across from us, he took a seat at his desk in the back of the room. We hadn't seen him since the Federal Council two days ago.

"I'm sorry; work's piled up. Do forgive me if I take care of some of it while we talk."

Fritz—who was the mayor of New York City, as well as a Tuner—opened up his computer and began typing busily.

"Is this cleanup from all those incidents?"

"...Yes. That's right, Fuubi Kase told me you'd resolved one just the other day." Glancing over at us for a moment, Fritz smiled. "I appreciate your help."

We were talking about the terrorist incidents that had occurred here in the city with the goal of having the Phantom Thief released. As the mayor, Fritz was having a tough time dealing with all of them.

"She's as much of a busybody as ever." Smiling wryly, he took a gentle dig at Ms. Fuubi. It had come up at the Federal Council, too; Ms. Fuubi had overstepped the boundaries of her job to help the Ace Detective, and now she was pursuing the Phantom Thief on her own.

"And?" Fritz asked, his pen kept skimming over the documents in front of him. "I was told you'd made a discovery in this string of Phantom Thief–related incidents."

Exactly: That was why we were here to see him.

"Yeah, actually. We know where he is."

The moment I said it, Fritz's hand stopped moving. He looked up, frowning while seeming perplexed. "You already know where the escaped Phantom Thief is?"

"Hey, don't underestimate the Ace Detective and her assistant." ...Although it had taken a hint from another Tuner for us to reach that answer.

"Tell me, then." Fritz's emerald eyes were focused on us. "Where is Phantom Thief Arsène now?"

"Right here," I told him bluntly.

Siesta was holding up a small round hand mirror. The mirror reflected a man whose eyes were as cold as ice, something even he probably hadn't been aware of.

"—I'm the Phantom Thief? That's quite the joke." Averting his eyes from his reflection, Fritz went back to typing. "I introduced myself just the other day. My name is Fritz, and my position is Revolutionary."

He rejected our conclusion without even meeting our eyes.

"No, you aren't Fritz Stewart. After all…" Siesta put the mirror away. "Fritz Stewart *is dead*. You, the Phantom Thief, have taken the deceased Revolutionary's place."

Fritz Stewart the Revolutionary was dead. Scarlet had told us as much last night. Then, who was the guy we'd met at the council two days ago? The vampire was a rogue who generally steered clear of the mundane world and didn't put in appearances at Federal Councils, and apparently, he hadn't known there was an impostor around.

Still, one thing was certain: *Somebody* had assumed the Revolutionary's identity and attended the council.

"In that case, hypothetically, let's say Fritz Stewart is a *fake*." Fritz—or rather, the man who'd called himself by that name—stopped typing entirely. "How can you be sure his true identity is the Phantom Thief?"

That was a perfectly natural question. If I said, "Because it would be easiest for a fellow Tuner to take his place," nobody would buy it. However, there was a reason that sort of switch would be easy for the Phantom Thief.

"Because the Phantom Thief can take on Fritz's shape using a seed."

That was what I'd guessed Seed had paid Arsene for stealing the sacred text. Then Arsene had taken the form of Fritz, his fellow Tuner, and had *stolen the position* of Revolutionary.

"Not only that, but the fact that none of the other Tuners have noticed the switch is proof in and of itself." Siesta gave another reason to believe that the fake Fritz was actually Arsene. "You've passed yourself off as Fritz Stewart for an entire month. You've attended the Federal Council, an assembly of Tuners, and boldly acted as mediator. Even so, none of the others—myself included—noticed that the Revolutionary was an impostor.

*The only conceivable explanation is because of your transcendental ability as the Phantom Thief."*

Siesta wasn't being overconfident in her own powers of observation or in those of the other Tuners. The group had dealt with many, many global crises, and their skills were definitely up to the task. Even then, not one of them had suspected that the Revolutionary's position had been stolen—because they'd been up against the Phantom Thief.

*"If Arsene steals from someone, that person will never notice."*

It was just as Siesta had said last night.

"I see. And you noticed it because you were the Singularity—or perhaps that would be a bit too simplistic."

The man was still seated at his desk. Assuming a faint, somewhat composed smile, he went on.

"Then, why do you suppose I needed to take over Fritz's identity?"

His tone was soft. Mellow, warm, and pleasant. That gentle voice enveloped me, and for a moment, I didn't even register the change in the way he spoke. It was completely different from the cold tone I'd heard several times at the council. This was his real voice.

"—Assistant."

I snapped back to reality with the force of a bursting water balloon.

My partner was right next to me, and I remembered what I needed to do. Right: This guy had just confessed that he was Phantom Thief Arsene. ...And yet he was still calmly trying to get us to tell him *his motive for switching.*

"Phantom Thief Arsene," Siesta said, although the man still wore Fritz's shape. "You changed your form and took over Fritz Stewart's identity—so that you could use the media to brainwash people around the world."

That might only be a theory. However, it was true that Arsene had a special skill that let him control people. Meaning it wasn't a stretch to assume he'd taken over Fritz's life in order to spread his voice around the world and exercise that power to its maximum potential.

"—I see," Arsene murmured, although it almost sounded like a sigh. Then silence fell.

"Let me clarify just one thing to avoid any misunderstandings." Arsene was the one who broke that silence. He placed both elbows on the desk, steepling his fingers in front of his chin. "I had absolutely no part in Fritz Stewart's death. He *just happened to die at a convenient time*, so I took his place, that's all." His voice was like being surrounded by soft ripples as he insisted he hadn't been involved in the man's death.

"Then, what are you after?" Siesta rose from her seat and stood in front of him. This time, she wasn't asking why the Phantom Thief had taken the Revolutionary's place. We'd deduced that correctly. "Fritz Stewart died a month ago, but he seems to have been making consistent media appearances still. Meaning you must have broken out of jail at least a month ago and have been living as the Revolutionary ever since. ...So, why?" she asked. "You've been free all this time. Why have you been manipulating complete strangers into attempting to release you?"

That was the question we'd shot down as impossible while we were out last night. If he'd been able to escape whenever he wanted, then there was no point in going out of his way to choose collaborators outside prison.

However, not only had Arsene been able to flee at any time; he'd already been aboveground and free a month ago. So why had he been making people in London and New York try to break him out of prison for no reason whatsoever?

In response to that completely natural question, Arsene said, "The fact that there is no point is, to me, the greatest point there is."

His answer was incomprehensible; it sounded like a Zen koan. Siesta and I both looked confused. Arsene watched us. "Don't you understand?"

"It's an experiment. To what extent are people able to do meaningless things on someone else's orders?"

It was a thought experiment that seemed to exist beyond the realm of reason. To Siesta, whose ideas were underpinned by solid experience and logic, that sort of thing was anathema. The phantom thief and the detective: Like spear and shield, they'd been at odds with each other since time immemorial and were destined to fight.

"Do you think we're going to let you continue that experiment?"

In that relationship, the detective was sometimes the one who took the offensive. Siesta, who'd risen to her feet along with me, pointed her familiar musket at the enemy.

"Rest assured." Paying no attention to the muzzle that was pointed at him, Arsene continued in a leisurely voice. "The experiment is over; I've collected sufficient statistics. I'm sure they'll get me through to the next stage."

"Look, there is no 'next'—"

"Besides…" Arsene got to his feet, cutting me off. "What the primordial seed gave me was only *a fragment* of a seed. I'm unlikely to develop unwanted side effects, but in exchange, its function is limited. That means, as it stands, I won't be able to maintain this shape. I'll have to go soon."

"…A fragment of a seed? You broke the Federal Charter and stole the sacred text for that?"

For some reason, Arsene seemed disappointed with my question. "I never let those I steal from realize what I've taken, yet you know I stole the primordial seed's sacred text. Doesn't that strike you as odd? You two were just telling me about this," Arsene scolded us.

He was right. We did know Arsene had stolen the text. However, that was because Siesta and Mia had set up the theft beforehand, so it hadn't seemed particularly strange…

"Don't tell me—are you saying the sacred text wasn't all you stole that day?" Still holding Arsene at gunpoint, Siesta cross-examined him, keeping him pinned down.

"…I see. So you had another objective?"

Siesta and Mia had realized Arsene was planning to steal the sacred text. They were on high alert. Even so, he had slipped through their guard and stolen *something else*—without letting them catch on.

"Then, all along, your real aim was…"

Siesta's blue eyes narrowed. She'd finally realized. She and Mia had thought they were using Arsene, but they were the ones who'd been used.

"Idly accepting what I'm owed isn't in my nature. When I really want something, I steal it myself."

Then he walked right past us.

"You think you can escape?" Copying Siesta, I pointed my gun at the enemy.

"Escape? I've never considered 'escaping' from anyone. Not even once." I heard an unsettling *click* right by my ear. "It's just that no one ever manages to catch up to me."

Out of the corner of my eye, I saw shiny black guns. Men had appeared out of nowhere, and both Siesta and I had guns pointed at the backs of our heads. We had no choice but to put our hands up.

"...Are you manipulating these guys, too?" From the way they were dressed, they seemed to be city employees. Arsene was probably controlling them with his ability—

"No." Arsene stopped walking for a moment. "They're all helping me of their own free will."

Leaving that screwy explanation behind, he headed for the door.

"I'm fairly sure you heard me earlier." However, a lone girl stopped him. Men in suits had her at gunpoint, but Siesta spoke over her shoulder to our departing enemy.

"A new Ace Detective will be taking over for me soon. Her passion is bound to capture you someday. Nagisa Natsunagi would never lose to the sort of enemy who uses human hearts."

In response to the Ace Detective's declaration of war, the Phantom Thief said...

"I'll look forward to stealing that passion."

He delivered that final remark with excitement, and then he was gone.

## ◆ Those dazzling three years I spent with her

After our showdown with the Phantom Thief, Siesta and I stopped by a restaurant instead of heading straight back to our hotel. We'd planned to hold a review meeting about our failure to capture Arsene over dinner, but...

"Take it easy, Siesta."

Where in that thin body of hers did all the food she ate go? Siesta cleaned plate after plate with lovely table manners but at dizzying speed. We had no time to talk about Arsene.

"But, you know, I need to eat while I can."

"What was the 'you know' for? You can eat again whenever you want."

Siesta wasn't listening. She was scanning the menu again. I was slightly exasperated...but it did also strike me as sort of nostalgic.

Back when we were together constantly, we'd eaten at the same table like this all the time, discussing cases or making plans for future work or talking about nothing in particular... Anyway, the sight I remembered most from those three years might have been Siesta blissfully enjoying her food, the same way she was doing that now.

"Come to think of it, what's your favorite food, Kimi?" she asked out of nowhere while we were waiting for our next order to arrive.

"Uh, what? Is there a reason you're talking like we just met?"

"No, it just occurred to me that we'd never discussed things like that."

I see. Come to think of it, she was right. It felt like we'd never talked about stuff like that or covered any of the basic topics; we'd just bantered.

"Actually, I don't even know your real name or age or where you're from."

"If you put it that way, I've practically never heard what you really think, Kimi."

Yeah, she wasn't wrong about that. Even if we hadn't asked those questions, though, we'd walked together and sometimes stood back-to-back, and we'd understood each other. I'd also never considered whether that had been right or wrong.

"Basically, I like anything that has a deep, rich flavor."

That wasn't why I said it, and it seemed kind of late, but I answered Siesta's question anyway.

"Deep, rich-tasting foods? That's not even a type."

"The thing is, as long as it has a definite taste, it satisfies me."

Especially during those three years, almost everything I ate had been pizza or some other kind of junk food. ...Maybe that was why. My strong memories with Siesta had been the only ones I'd remembered, as if they were linked to those vivid flavors.

"What about you, Siesta?"

"Mm, that's a tough one. There's nothing I dislike."

As she answered, Siesta paused in the act of reaching for her glass. Thinking back, I did get the feeling she found everything she ate delicious. The only time she'd grimaced was when I'd made that lousy curry... Maybe she really didn't have any favorites.

"If I were having my very last supper, though..." Siesta responded to my inquiry with a hypothetical. "I think I'd like to eat it with the person I most enjoy spending time with." Smiling faintly, she gave an answer that didn't quite match the original question.

"...I ate too much."

Still fully dressed, I collapsed onto the hotel bed.

"Heh-heh. Yes, your stomach's definitely sticking out."

Siesta had cleared more plates than I had, but it was like everything she'd eaten had evaporated or something. She sat down in a chair by the window, wearing a cool smile. We'd finally finished our long dinner and returned to our hotel. ...Speaking of *finally*, there was one more thing.

"Still, that wasn't like you. You never back down that easily." On the bed, gazing at the ceiling, I brought up the Arsène incident again. A few hours ago, surrounded by those men in that office, Siesta and I had ended up letting the Phantom Thief get away.

"I didn't know how Arsène had gotten those men to obey him. I couldn't use force."

...Oh, I see. If we hadn't withdrawn, there was no telling what *order* he would have given them. To ensure the safety of everyone present, she'd had to pretend she was helpless.

"Besides, even if I lost, *the Ace Detective hasn't*," Siesta said firmly. "Someday, Nagisa's bound to defeat the Phantom Thief."

"...Yeah. Now we've got another reason we have to wake her up." There was no way she'd let an enemy who plotted to control others' hearts get away.

Nagisa Natsunagi. With her passion, I was sure…

"But as far as you're concerned, Kimi, that's not the biggest reason." I heard the bed creak. Straddling me, Siesta peered into my face. "You just want to wake Nagisa up because you want to see her again."

"…Don't just say people's thoughts aloud. At least ask first."

"I'm right, though, aren't I?"

The room was dim. The moonlight that filtered in through the curtains made Siesta's smile even more alluring.

"…Dunno." I knew there was no need to put her off. Even so, it was awkward to be seen so thoroughly, and I found myself looking away.

"Male *tsunderes* aren't popular, you know."

"Mind your own business."

Today, though, Siesta wouldn't let up. "Tell me one thing you like about her, then."

*What's the "then" for, huh?* Actually, something like this happened just three weeks ago. …In which case, it wouldn't be fair if I didn't answer this time, too.

"…Natsunagi, right. Well, you know. She's, uh……cute, isn't she?"

"………"

Why did she clam up? Should I have mentioned her personality first or something?

"Oh, it's just that hearing the word 'cute' come out of your mouth gave me a nasty chill."

"Not fair." *That's not a reason to get goosebumps.* I plucked up my courage and said something I don't normally say. *Praise me for it, would ya?*

"Heh-heh. Still, this is getting entertaining."

"Don't tease me for your own amusement. Whatever it is, it's obviously not going to be any fun for me."

"Well, it means that even when Nagisa called you names or brushed you off, in your heart, you were thinking, *My partner is way too cute,* right?"

"Quit analyzing it so calmly! And I didn't make that 'cool guy' face!"

…*Dammit, Natsunagi. Thanks to you, I'm getting humiliated here.*

"Yes, right there, that's the one I meant."

"Like I said, quit reading my mind."

*And you. Hurry up and get off me already.* I pointed at the bed next to mine, instructing Siesta to move. *Man, I'm glad we reserved a twin room.*

"...Uh, you're interpreting that gesture wrong." For some reason, instead of going to the next bed, the ace detective had stretched out next to me. Had she always been this slow on the uptake?

"Oh, of course. I didn't realize."

Yeah, right. She'd clearly done it on purpose.

Speaking in a nonchalant monotone, Siesta gazed at my profile. Her face softened.

"What are you after?" I asked.

"You wouldn't stop talking about Nagisa, so I got jealous... Would that do?"

"If you'd put more emotion into it, I might have hugged you out of nowhere."

"You didn't put any emotion into that either, Kimi."

We argued a little, then laughed.

"We haven't changed, have we?"

"Nope. We're just like we were a year ago."

The lights in the room were out. On the narrow bed, Siesta and I gazed at each other.

"Well, your drive for sleep and food have been satisfied, so if we're being honest, I'm concerned you might hit me up for *the last one*."

"I told you, I've only got two great motivations. And what do you mean, 'concerned'?" Siesta narrowed her eyes as if she had a bone to pick with me.

"You say that now, but that's not what you said before."

"When?"

It had been a month ago already. When we fought Chameleon on that cruise ship, and Siesta had borrowed Natsunagi's body, she'd told me...

"You said, 'To tell you the truth, I might have slept with you once. I considered it, at least.'"

"............" For a moment, Siesta looked rather guilty. "...Well, you said to tell you that sooner, didn't you? Really, it sounded as if you were the one who was interested."

She hit me with an impossible instant retort.

*Well, back then, I had no idea I'd get to see you again like this.*

"And so, if I had to say, I thought *you* might not be able to control your emotions seeing me again after a year apart, and you'd throw your arms around me or something." Somehow having gotten the upper hand, Siesta reproached me. ...Sheesh.

"Get over yourself." She was lying next to me, and I geared up to flick her forehead.

"Well, I mean..." Suddenly, Siesta's expression turned lonely. "You pushed yourself much too hard for my sake." She gently touched my cheek.

...Oh. So she had known about that seed, huh?

"Even if the seed's been extracted, you might still end up suffering side effects from it one of these days." Was it my imagination? Siesta's eyes seemed wet. "You may lose the ability to see your beloved Nagisa or hear your cherished Yui sing. You may lose your voice; you might not be able to fight with your rival Charlie. Even so, you—"

"I don't care," I said, hugging her tightly. "I knew I wouldn't. That's why I chose the future that might have you in it." No matter what I lost because of it, I'd wanted to see Siesta again. "Sorry. I just said I hadn't changed, but I've learned how to be honest about stuff like that."

I'd failed to do it twice, and I had regretted it both times.

"...Are you stupid, Kimi?" I could hear Siesta's weak voice from the vicinity of my chest. "That almost sounds as if you..."

But she didn't say the rest of it. She just squirmed a little in my arms... then heaved a big sigh. "I suspect somebody's going to stab you one day."

"Where the heck did that come from?" Even if I am a trouble magnet, I never want to get dragged into that kind of mess.

"Listen." Siesta poked her head up out of my arms. There was no sadness in her face now. "Come to think of it, I didn't ask you last time. I think you'd probably tell me now." With that preface, Siesta asked me, "What did you think of those three years?"

That was another thing that had happened on the cruise ship a month ago. While Siesta was protecting me from the enemy's attacks, she'd told me, *"Those unforgettable three years I spent with you are the best memories I have."*

At the time, I hadn't been able to respond. Since she'd asked me again, I had a chance to tell her. In that case...

"Do you even need to ask?"

Knowing it was too dark for her to really see it anyway, I gave her my biggest smile.

"I had so much fun, it's kind of frustrating."

When she heard that, Siesta murmured, "I see." She sounded somewhat relieved. She put her arms around me, hugging me back. "Thank you."

Yeah, that's right.

That was the promise we'd made a year ago: If we survived and met again, I'd take her up on that hug.

Right now, one year later, that wish had come true.

"What's that 'Thank you' supposed to mean?" But as I joked around with her like usual, Siesta's warmth enfolded me. My eyelids grew heavy, and I didn't fight them. I fell into a deep sleep.

—The next morning...

When I woke up, I was alone.

# Chapter 3

## ◆ The true conclusion of Route X

"What do you mean, Ma'am's gone?!"

Furious, Charlie grabbed my shirtfront. Her blond hair was disheveled, and her sharp, angry eyes drilled into me.

"...It's just like I said." I didn't try to resist. I simply told her the facts. "Siesta left a letter saying she won't be coming back to us."

I thought back to yesterday morning. The moment I woke up, I'd realized Siesta wasn't lying next to me. Instead, there was a letter on the desk. It consisted of her usual banter, a simple thank-you for everything, and a goodbye.

Even though she'd spent day after day sleeping like a log until evening, when she vanished, it happened in the blink of an eye. I'd found a familiar musket leaning against the wall beside the bed. It was as if she was saying she wouldn't need it anymore.

Siesta's letter hadn't mentioned the most important thing: her reasons for leaving. ...No, technically, there had been something like that. She'd said since she was retiring as the Ace Detective and becoming a regular detective again, she was planning to do some solo traveling. I'd grown enough as an assistant, so she wanted me to support Natsunagi, who would be the new Ace Detective someday. The things she'd said were sound, difficult to argue with, *and that was why I instinctively felt they weren't true*. It wasn't just my gut; it was experience. The three years I'd spent with her were telling me so.

However, it was an undeniable fact that Siesta was no longer nearby. I'd returned to Japan before the day was up, taking only her musket with me, and today I'd gathered Charlie and the others so I could report the situation.

"—So you just looked at that letter and shuffled back home by yourself, when you didn't even understand what Ma'am really wanted? Then you haven't changed at all in the past year, Kimizuka!"

"Please calm down, Charlie!" A girl came between us, attempting to mediate. "Kimizuka, tell us one more time. Did Siesta really leave you...? Leave us?"

Saikawa turned her wavering eyes on me. We were in a certain room of her mansion.

"You're walking again. That's great."

Saikawa had been in a wheelchair until just the other day, but now she was standing firmly on her own two feet.

"Don't try to change the subject. Never mind me. About Siesta..." Saikawa put a little anger into her words, most likely gearing up to scold me...but then she didn't. "Kimizuka, you look terrible."

"Ha-ha. You're insulting me now?"

"You don't need to force yourself to joke. Please sit down." Saikawa motioned for me to have a seat.

"...Come to think of it, there were vague signs hinting this would happen." Lowering myself weakly into the chair, I told them about the things I'd thought on the way here. About how what Siesta had said and done lately had seemed a little off somehow.

For example, even though she'd come back to life, she kept saying things like "There's no time." She might have meant something besides needing to defeat Seed quickly or wake up Natsunagi.

Then, although she'd been expressing her anxieties to me, Siesta had taken me to a distant country, had put me in contact with new Tuners, invited me to musicals, and started reminiscing... I'd experienced a similar *contradiction* between her words and her actions a year ago, too.

Most of all, she'd stepped down from her position and nominated Natsunagi as the new Ace Detective. She'd said that even if she didn't hold that title anymore, she'd keep working as an ordinary detective; however, if this was how things stood, her retirement took on a different meaning.

"Siesta might be—"

"——! That can't be right!" After she'd heard me out, Charlie looked down and screamed. "Ma'am really came back to life! We finally defeated Seed! Nagisa will wake up after this, and then we'll finally make it to that happy ending you were talking about, you know?! And now Ma'am... Ma'am disappears again, all by herself?! That can't be...!"

"Your deduction may be correct, Kimihiko."

Just then, someone else came in. It was Noches, the former maid-type SIESTA; she'd had business to take care of, and she apologized for being late. Then she began to relate a story that seemed to reinforce my theory. "As Charlotte says, the primordial seed has been destroyed. However, the *fragments of his seed* are still here—Including inside Mistress Siesta's chest."

...She was right. Saikawa, Natsunagi, and I had all had our seeds extracted during that battle with Seed the other day, but Siesta's was still in her heart. Up until now, she'd benefited from the power it gave her, fighting the enemies of the world using physical abilities no average person had.

"However, those seeds are double-edged swords. As nourishment, they take the sight or hearing, or part of the life, from anyone who ingests one. And eventually—"

"Wait!" Saikawa hastily cut Noches off. "We know the rest. Albert told us what happens to humans who've been eroded by a seed. But Siesta was originally Seed's candidate vessel, wasn't she? Then—"

"...I see. So Siesta wasn't fully compatible," I said.

Noches nodded quietly.

Before Siesta and Mia plotted to deceive Seed, the sacred text had originally foretold a future in which Siesta lost to Hel. That told us one thing: As a vessel for the primordial seed, Hel had been a little better than Siesta.

"As the sole fully compatible host for the primordial seed, Nagisa Natsunagi might have—"

A remark Stephen the Inventor had made in passing a week ago ran through my mind. Natsunagi had been the one best suited to be Seed's vessel, while Siesta's body was doomed to be eaten away by the seed in her heart—

"Don't tell me Ma'am is…"

Charlie cut to the heart of it.

"Is she trying to disappear before she turns into a monster?"

People whose bodies were completely devoured by their seeds *degraded.* Like Chameleon, who'd lost control when we fought him on the cruise ship, or Betelgeuse, who'd been created as a biological weapon to begin with. That was how those who were controlled by the seeds ended up.

Siesta had known it would happen to her one day, and so she'd left us before she ran out of time.

"Wait just a minute. If Ma'am knows she'll become a monster someday… If it's true…"

She didn't have to say what Siesta would do.

Before that could happen, she'd—

"……!"

Charlie bolted for the door.

"Where are you going?"

"You have to ask?! I'm going to find Ma'am!"

"She's—!" I'd shouted, although I hadn't meant to, and Charlie's shoulders jumped. "She understood all of that, and she chose to do this."

"But even so! Just because she knows she'll become a monster someday, *suicide isn't the—!*"

"Not that," I said to Charlie but kept my eyes fixed on the floor. "Siesta knows how much we cared about her and how happy it made us to see her again. And *knowing all of that,* she still chose this."

"……!"

That meant we were dealing with an entirely different situation now.

True, we'd brought Siesta back by superseding her will and her intentions. However, Siesta knew about our feelings this time. On top of that, she'd decided that this was the only way and had distanced herself from us. We couldn't just ignore her silent wish.

"It's all right. For now, calm down."

My hand felt something warm.

"Your hands squeeze. Your shoulders roll. Your breathing is rhythmic. Close your eyes, take a deep breath, then exhale. Your blood circulates. When you open your eyes, your cloudy vision will be clear."

It was Saikawa's usual charm. My hand hung limply, and she took it gently. "Siesta has made her decision. Now it's your turn to choose, Kimizuka."

She'd removed her eye patch, and the eyes she fixed on me were two different colors.

"…It's still okay for me to choose?"

"Of course. It's your life, after all." For some reason, Saikawa's smile seemed ready to dissolve into tears.

Still, considering the fact that my ego had created this situation, I couldn't answer so easily.

"We were always like this, weren't we?" Charlie looked away, murmuring sadly. "In battle we'd argue, and so of course we'd fail, and then we'd get along worse and do the whole thing over again."

She was right. Every time that happened, Siesta would scold us, sighing and asking if we were stupid. Even so, in the end, she'd smile and point us in the right direction. …But Siesta wasn't here anymore. All because of my selfish wish.

"Sorry, Charlotte."

The one who'd pointed us toward tomorrow was no longer—

"We still have a detective!" Angrily, or possibly through tears, Charlie stomped over to me. Setting her hands on my shoulders, she shouted, "We have another friend who's a detective! She said so herself that day. She said she was the ace detective who'd inherited Ma'am's last wish!"

What I'd seen on that cruise ship flashed through my mind. At the time, Charlie had adamantly refused to acknowledge Natsunagi as the ace detective. She'd thought she was the most suitable one to inherit Siesta's last wish.

Just now, though, Charlie had entrusted it to her. She'd entrusted our future—Siesta's future—to the other ace detective. The one who was still asleep.

"Kimihiko," Noches called. She was holding a car key.

Would I find the answer in the place where Natsunagi slept? Wouldn't we just come up against another harsh reality—? I didn't know.

"If you don't know, then let's go."

Noches, whose consciousness had once been housed in Siesta's body, spoke to me over her shoulder. I sensed the shadow of the ace detective in her, and before I knew it, I'd stepped forward.

## ◆ Client and proxy detective

When I opened the door of the hospital room, the girl was lying on the bed, just as she had been before.

"I'm back," I told her, gazing at her sleeping face.

It had been two weeks since the final battle with Seed, and Nagisa Natsunagi still showed no sign of waking.

"I guess it wasn't going to be this convenient, huh…?"

Saikawa and Charlie had encouraged me to come here, but Natsunagi still hadn't awakened. No miracles had occurred. Even so, I wanted to talk to her about this, so I sat down in a nearby chair.

It had been four days since my last visit. I had come to this hospital room several times before I left for New York, and during those visits, I'd *scolded* her a lot. She'd tried to sacrifice herself in Siesta's place, and as her assistant, I—and no one else—had to yell at her for it.

"Do you get it, Natsunagi?"

Looking at her still face made me think of it again, and I couldn't help but complain to her. *I said I wanted to revive Siesta, but you know it's not okay for you to be gone instead.*

My anger didn't faze her, though. Natsunagi kept on sleeping and breathing peacefully.

"…Natsunagi, what do you think I should do?"

A sigh escaped me. The red ribbon beside her pillow caught my eye.

Siesta had come back to life, and in her place, Natsunagi had died. Even so, Natsunagi had inherited Alicia's and Hel's lives and wills and returned to us once—but now here she was again, asleep. Meanwhile, Siesta had left us and was probably attempting to disappear from the world entirely.

"What is it with you people?"

Why did they play with my heart like this? Why make me worry?

Why couldn't they both just stay safe? Why couldn't they just smile and be well and happy?

*You ace detectives are always—*

"—No, I know. I know I'm in the wrong here."

The whole reason Natsunagi had ended up like this was because I'd misjudged her determination. I'd wanted to bring Siesta back to life no matter what it would have cost me, and Natsunagi had wanted the exact same thing...and yet...

Then there was Siesta. She'd had that seed inside her, but I hadn't thought about what that might mean for her. I'd brought her back to life due to my own selfish thoughts, and this was the result. She was trying to disappear before she could turn into a monster.

"Just two weeks."

That was the amount of time I'd managed to spend with her. Even then, we'd hardly gotten to talk during the first week, since we'd spent it in the hospital recovering after our fight with Seed. Ultimately, what I'd gained from sacrificing all those things was a few days' worth of memories to ease my regrets and the sorrow of a second parting.

"What should I do, Natsunagi?"

I knew she wouldn't answer, but I asked again anyway. I'd been able to tell Siesta things I hadn't managed to tell her before, and she'd accepted my feelings...but she still chose to leave us.

Saikawa had told me that if that was Siesta's choice, it was fine for me to make choices of my own. ...But was it really? Not that I thought Saikawa's advice was wrong, but...

I was just hesitant to second-guess Siesta again. Sure, I'd stuck to my guns and superseded her intentions once. But if this was the result, I had to admit it, no matter how reluctantly: Her call had been better than mine.

"I guess I've already got my answer, don't I?"

The mental back-and-forth I'd just had with myself helped everything fall into place. I'd been wrong, and Siesta had been right. I didn't even have to think about it. During those three years, not once had she been wrong.

...But on the day Siesta died a year ago, I'd had a thought. I wasn't proud of it; just this time, I'd wanted her to have been mistaken. Of course, that had been childish. I didn't need anybody to tell me that.

"—But I still want Siesta to live...!"

I knew full well that it was a mistake, that my wish was pure arrogance. It was as clear as it could be, but I couldn't think of any way to make it happen now. I bit my lip. My nails dug into my palms. There was still nothing we could do about the current situation, and my vision went black.

"...What should I do, Ace Detective?"

If biting my lip wasn't going to change anything, I needed to at least ask the question.

That's right. I'd been devastated before I came here, but Charlie had told me off for it and encouraged me. She'd said if I couldn't find the answer, I should rely on the other ace detective.

That's why I was clinging to her, even though I knew I wasn't right. If digging my fingernails into my palms wouldn't change anything, then at least—

"Please, Ace Detective. Save Siesta."

Releasing my clenched, rigid fists, I squeezed Natsunagi's left hand.

"If you'll settle for a proxy detective, I'll take the job."

Out of nowhere, I heard a familiar voice.

It sounded like the exchange we'd had that one time, in that classroom bathed in the light from the sunset.

Actually, maybe I'd been the one who'd said it or something like it.

The hand I was holding squeezed mine back.

"You held my hand like this before, didn't you?"

When I lifted my head, the girl was gazing at me. She smiled with relief.

Those words reminded me of another day. I'd held her hand that night in the hospital, over a year ago, when she still looked like Alicia.

"Natsu...nagi...?" My voice was hoarse, but I managed to say her name somehow.

Looking up at me from the bed, Natsunagi gave a wry smile. "You sure are dumb, Kimizuka."

Slowly releasing my hand, she flicked my forehead with her middle finger.

"Don't visit me in the hospital, then spend the whole time talking about some other girl."

## ◆ Setting Nagisa in motion

"Natsunagi..."

Dazed, I called her name again.

Nagisa Natsunagi—a girl in my grade and my partner. Death had separated us once, or so I'd thought. Then she'd spent almost an eternity asleep. And now here she was, blinking right in front of me.

"Yes, my name is Nagisa Natsunagi. ...Heh-heh. It's been a while, huh?" Slowly sitting up, she flashed a goofy smile and a peace sign at me. "...Huh? Kimizuka, are you crying? Ah-ha-ha! I guess you reeeeally wanted to see me, didn't—?"

I hugged her as hard as I could.

"Wait, what? ...Huh? K-Kimizuka...?"

Natsunagi's flustered voice was right by my ear, but I couldn't afford to glance at her face or ask how she was doing. I wanted to stay like this forever, if she'd let me.

"Wow, I really didn't expect this... Um, Kimizuka? ...What in the...?" Bewildered, Natsunagi became stiff and awkward. "Listen, I think you're

breaking character. You're not normally the type for this sort of thing, are you?"

"…Shut up."

It was no good. Speaking made my nose feel stuffy.

I hugged her tightly, so she couldn't see my face.

"…Oh, geez. Honestly. What are we going to do with you?"

A soft warmth enfolded my back.

Natsunagi was hugging me too.

"Oh, I see. Yes, of course. This was what you wanted, wasn't it?"

It was like a reenactment of the time I'd met Natsunagi in that classroom. Back then, she'd been hoping I'd step into the role of detective and find the owner of her heart. As a matter of fact, though, that heart had already gotten its wish, and Natsunagi had done what it wanted and held me close.

"Um, what was it again? Seriously, you're all tearstained and covered in snot, and you still want to cry and throw a tantrum? You had other ways you wanted to play? …I think that's how it went."

"……! You don't have to reenact that part!" I shook free of her arms, and we finally managed to look each other in the face.

"Pfft!"

"Heh."

Then we both burst out laughing.

How long had it been since I saw Natsunagi smile like this?

"Kimizuka, you look awful." She pointed at my red eyes. "You wanted to see me that bad, huh?" she teased.

"Yeah. I did," I replied. I told her how I genuinely felt. "I wanted to see you and make you bawl."

"…Mgh." Natsunagi must have known why already. She averted her eyes, looking guilty.

If Natsunagi woke up, I'd meant to scold her first thing. There was no way sacrificing her own life to save her friends was the right answer. That could never be the future everyone wanted. …But…

"It turns out I'm not in any position to lecture you." When I said that, Natsunagi looked at me again.

I couldn't deny that I might have done the same thing if I'd been in her shoes. As a matter of fact, I'd swallowed that seed, and I'd been prepared to sacrifice myself when I did it.

"I was so happy you were alive that I didn't feel like getting mad."

"...What's that supposed to mean?" Natsunagi gave an appalled little laugh. Then she wiped the tears from the corners of her eyes with her fingertips.

"But, Natsunagi, why did you suddenly wake up?" I had zero complaints, of course, but we couldn't just label this *coincidence* and be done with it. I asked her how this miracle had occurred.

"I wonder." Natsunagi looked away, gazing out the hospital room window. "The whole time I was unconscious, I was on a lovely shore. It wasn't dark, the way it used to be, and I wasn't in a birdcage that kept me from going anywhere. It was just the clear, blue ocean and the sort of white, sandy beach that makes you want to run down it barefoot. I stayed at the waterline, staring at the ocean."

It had to have been the world of Natsunagi's subconscious. Unlike the times when Hel had been in control of her mind, she must have felt she'd completed her mission. That beach was her mental image of her goal.

"But as I was staring at the ocean, a little hand thumped me on the back." Natsunagi placed her hand on the left side of her chest. "When I turned around, I saw a cute, doll-like girl who looked like she'd jumped straight out of Wonderland. She was desperately trying to tell me something, but for some reason, I couldn't hear her voice."

As Natsunagi remembered, she squeezed her hand into a tight fist over her chest and the heart inside it.

She must have known who was in there.

"Then, I heard *another girl's voice* from her mouth. That voice was also terribly familiar, an indivisible part of me...and the next thing I knew, I'd obeyed it and started to move."

...Yeah, that was how we'd always been. Both as our enemy and our ally, her voice had always set us in motion. *She*, the one who bore the name of the queen of the dead, had tried to push Natsunagi back to this world. Her *word-soul* power had spoken for the voiceless girl with pink hair.

"What did she say?" I asked.

Natsunagi raised her head.

"—She told me to start running."

Natsunagi's dignified expression wasn't one I'd ever seen her wear before. Her heart and memories and consciousness were home to many other people. I was sure that wholeheartedly accepting their wills had given her new life. The girl who'd agonized over her lack of identity was no longer there.

"After that, things seemed to happen so fast." Her expression softened. "Every cell in this body was screaming that it wanted to see you. So I ran across that shore, ran and ran, until I caught up...to you." Natsunagi bumped her fist lightly against my chest.

"Why me?"

"Well, you were hopelessly depressed. Even in my sleep, I could tell." Natsunagi smiled wryly.

"That's why you..."

I remembered what Scarlet had said that night: That human instinct was found in DNA all through the body, circulating like blood. That the dead he resurrected came back with that instinct intact.

I didn't know where in Natsunagi's body her mind or soul or consciousness slept, whether it was her brain or her heart or every single one of her cells. I did know exactly what her instinct was, though: her passion as a detective.

For ages, she hadn't been anyone. Then one day, when she'd inherited the role of detective, she'd found the path she was meant to walk. Sometimes she'd followed Siesta, and at others, she'd chosen a different course, but she'd never lost sight of her pride as a detective.

So when I, her client, had called out to her, Natsunagi the detective had responded by waking up. It was just like when we'd fought Chameleon on the ship. Siesta's mind had been dormant inside Natsunagi, but since I was in trouble, she'd awakened and stepped up. This time, Natsunagi had—

"I suspect you two like me far too much," I joked, feeling as if a great weight had lifted from my shoulders.

"So, about your current problem."

"......Hey."

Natsunagi chuckled, pulling the covers up to hide the lower half of her face. "Unfortunately, I don't like you or anything, Kimizuka."

*Yeah, I know that. It's mutual. I don't like you or Siesta one tiny bit, either.*

"But if you need us, we'll run to you, no matter where you are." Natsunagi looked at me with those ruby eyes of hers. "We'll ignore common sense, we'll color outside the lines, we'll replace the term *deus ex machina* with *miracle*, and we'll go to see you. ...If that's what you want."

Natsunagi spoke for the other detective, too—the one who wasn't with us.

"...Say, Natsunagi?"

"Hm?" She gazed at me kindly.

"Then, if I said I wanted to see Siesta one more time..."

"Of course!" Still sitting up in bed, she confidently planted her hands on her hips. "That's why you came here, isn't it?"

"...You knew, huh?"

That's just like an ace detective, I guess. Natsunagi said, "Pacing is important with stuff like this," echoing a line I'd heard somewhere before.

"Actually, I heard you when you were talking to yourself earlier."

"...Then wake up sooner." I'd gone and looked like a coward for nothing.

"Basically, Kimizuka, you're not sure whether it's okay to reject Siesta's answer again, right?"

Yeah, that's the one. Siesta knew everything regarding how we felt and what we wished for. Was it okay to overrule the decision she'd made, even then, for the sake of my own selfish wish?

"In that case..." Natsunagi's voice cut through my hesitation. "Why not just stop relying on uncertain things like feelings and wishes?"

Voluntarily discarding her passion, her greatest weapon, she said:

"Let's work together and supersede Siesta one more time. Not just with emotion—but with genuine skill."

Thus our war council for transcending the ace detective began.

## ◆ Where this muzzle points

After the discussion with Natsunagi, I'd done all I could to get ready—and the next day, I left for a certain neighborhood.

"It's hardly changed at all."

Stepping over the yellow police tape, I entered the abandoned town. I walked along, careful not to trip on the cracked ground, until finally I saw a great tree, larger than the rest. It was the one that had swallowed up the shopping mall.

This was the city that had been overrun by plants, the one where we'd fought Seed two weeks ago. Many of the buildings had collapsed, and there was Do Not Cross tape all over the place; normal civilians weren't allowed to enter. I was there for just one reason.

"Hey, what a coincidence," I shouted.

I'd spoken to a lone girl who had her back to me.

She was standing there, looking up at that huge tree. Short, pale silver hair, and a dress inspired by a military uniform. Everything about her was unmistakable: The girl's name was—

"What are you doing, Siesta?"

Apparently, she'd had time to prepare because when she turned back, she was wearing her usual composed smile. "I didn't think we'd meet again, Assistant."

Code name: Siesta.

My partner had disappeared and turned up again.

"Geez. What are you, a cat?"

They say a pet cat who senses its death approaching will leave its owner before it dies.

"And who exactly is claiming to own me?" Siesta responded with a cold, hard stare. Then she gave a dissatisfied sigh. "It appears someone set me up."

Tilting her head back to look up at the towering tree, she murmured, "I heard that the seal on the primordial seed was coming undone."

That had been one of the things I'd done in preparation. If I was going to talk Siesta around, I had to find her first, but I knew there was no point in calling and asking to see her. In that case, I thought, *it would be better to summon the Ace Detective* instead of Siesta.

Natsunagi hadn't taken over that position yet. That meant Siesta was still the Ace Detective, and the last thing she'd ever do was abandon a job. So I'd made Mia Whitlock the Oracle *lie* that there were signs that Seed's seal was breaking, which would lure her to this place.

"They do say it could happen someday."

"Then, at the very least, it's not an immediate danger."

"Right. As a matter of fact, it may end up being indispensable to mankind." I told her what I'd just heard from Ms. Fuubi the night before. "They tell me that tree is emitting unidentified atoms that don't appear in the periodic table. They're going to be real busy analyzing those."

That was the main reason this area had been cordoned off. What would this great tree, the primordial seed's seal, mean for humanity's future?

"I see. Then there's nothing for me to do here. That's good," Siesta said, attempting to end this conversation. This story.

"What's 'good,' huh?" As she turned to go, I called after her. "Are you planning to die?"

She stopped in her tracks.

"In the not-so-distant future, I'll turn into a monster."

Siesta turned around to face me. Her smile looked a little lonely.

"I first realized I might not be the primordial seed's most compatible vessel when I saw a sacred text that had been written long ago. I understood that the seed lying dormant inside me might begin to eat away at me one day."

"…You're telling me that for those three years we traveled together, you were holding that bomb all by yourself?"

"My seed is in my heart. Maybe that's why I'm vaguely aware of its *time limit. For now*, I'm still okay, but *that day* is inevitable." Siesta placed her hand on the left side of her chest. "In the near future—I'll stop being able to see or hear you. Even though you've been beside me the whole time. I'll lose the voice I'd need to fight with you. I'll forget you, and…someday, I'll kill you. And so…" Even at a time like this, Siesta's smile was beautiful. "I'm going to leave this world before that happens."

That was my assumption. I didn't need to be right. I hadn't wanted it to be. But Siesta's own words had just erased all doubt.

"Your feelings really did make me happy." As I stood there, silent, Siesta went on eloquently. "The only words I can find are simple ones, but I was happy. You got angry for my sake. You cried for me. And so I'm sure…I was happy."

An ace detective was brilliant, calm, cool, and collected. As such, Siesta sometimes prioritized logic over emotion. She emptied her heart, exclusively pursuing results. I was aware of that, so what she'd just said sounded like her genuine, unexaggerated feelings.

"Then are you saying you have no regrets?"

It was an incredibly cruel question, but I asked it anyway.

"I might have had some last year." Siesta's pale silver hair fluttered in the wind. She gave a small, crooked smile. "I still had things I wanted to ask you then. But…" She tucked her hair behind her ears. "I know you consider me precious now. I know you enjoyed those three years. Then, even though I never expected to, I got to go to your apartment again and have pizza with you…and then fight the enemy, travel by air, and solve a case, and see a musical, and hold you close. I have no more regrets."

Siesta spoke firmly. I saw no hesitation in her face.

In that case, my answer was—

"So why are you trying to stop me?"

*I'd drawn my gun,* and Siesta gave me a piercing, cold stare.
"Sorry for being an assistant who doesn't do what you want."
*I came here to stop you. Not to kill you or hurt you.* I was pointing my gun at Siesta in order to protect her, to keep her alive.
"Who says I have to play along with you?"
Siesta turned a deaf ear to my resolution. That was only natural. Why should she go out of her way to deal with my rebellion? There was nothing in it for her. If I lowered my gun, or if the conversation trailed off, Siesta would leave us forever—even so...
"There's no point in running. I'll chase after you no matter what it takes, even if it means using the Saikawa family fortune or borrowing help from Charlie's old unit. The ends of the earth, the depths of the ocean, ten thousand meters up—I'll follow you everywhere."
After all, the Ace Detective hated to give up—but I could give her a run for her money.
"And if that sounds like too much trouble, I should fight you here?" Gazing down the barrel of my gun, Siesta guessed at what I was implying.
"That's right. We'll settle everything here. If you win, I won't mess with you anymore."
"There's no way you and I could have anything resembling an actual fight, and you know it. Besides—" Siesta turned her back to me, calling my bluff. "You and your friends can pursue me all you want, but you'll never catch me. I'll find a deserted place and time, and I'll complete my story by myself." After giving that remark, she started to leave.
Where had Siesta's story as the ace detective begun? Had it been when she was born, or was it at that laboratory six years ago, when her battle with the primordial seed was established? I was only her assistant, and I didn't know.

But when had *my* story as her assistant begun? Or what about our story, Siesta's and mine? ...I knew that one for sure. It was that day. That one day, four years ago.

"Oh, I see. Siesta, you..."

What I had to say here and now had been determined back then.

"You got scared of me, your assistant. You're pretending the match has already been settled without a fight, so you can force me to admit a loss and end the game. In other words—you're afraid."

The moment I said it, Siesta stopped in her tracks. There was no way she'd forgotten whose taunt that had originally been and when it was from.

"Are you stupid, Kimi?"

She reproached me the way she always did.

But on this battlefield, her voice seemed just a little energized.

"It's a thousand years too early for you to provoke me."

When she turned back to face me, she was holding a small pistol in her left hand. "Come to think of it, we've never really tried to kill each other before, have we?"

"No, although you single-handedly almost killed me."

Even under these circumstances—no, because of them—Siesta and I smiled at each other.

"—Now then."

But almost immediately, our eyes turned cold.

"Are you ready for this, Siesta?"

"I could ask you the same, Assistant."

Then, at the foot of the great tree towering over all mankind, Siesta and I pointed our guns at each other.

"You'll never
stop me."

"I swear I'll
stop you."

It was the first—and last—big fight we ever had.

## ◆ The name of this feeling

"In that case, I won't hold back."

No sooner had Siesta murmured those words than she *vanished*.

"......!"

I knew better than anyone on the planet how strong she was. Siesta ran so fast, she might as well have been teleporting. Choosing a random direction, I dodged, and almost immediately, a gunshot rang out right next to me.

"I guess it's not going to be possible to end you with just one shot."

I had the devil's luck and had won out this time; I might be rolling on the ground, but I'd dodged that bullet. I took cover behind an abandoned bus. "Couldn't you have given me a bit of a head start?"

"There is no 'time out' in war. Never mind that. What do I have to do to win this fight?"

"Look, don't fire, and then confirm things afterward. ...You win if I admit I lost."

"I see. Then we'll call it a battle against time. Considering your personality, though, I get the feeling this may drag on for quite a while."

Siesta wasn't even entertaining the possibility she might lose. Not only that, but she'd tacitly managed to insult me for not knowing when to quit.

"Sorry, but I'm flipping our power dynamic today." I fired from behind the bus...but Siesta evaded with an acrobatic leap.

"Aiming for my legs. That's kind of you."

"No, it's just not normal to aim for my head first thing like you did."

"But you won't admit defeat unless I inflict a lethal injury, will you?"

Even as we traded this combat-specific banter, I got my breathing under control behind the bus, working out a strategy. This place had been messed up nicely during the fight with Seed two weeks ago, so at least I'd secured cover.

"Do you think you can beat me like that?"

"......!"

I'd just tripped my own death flag. I heard the Ace Detective's voice above me. Siesta had gotten up onto the bus's roof and jumped off with no hesitation, kicking my right arm hard and knocking the pistol out of my hand.

"…! As a matter of fact, I did supersede your intentions once, remember?" Without even glancing at the gun I'd dropped, I ducked under the bus.

"In terms of feelings, yes. Unless you can beat me with actual skill right now, there's no point."

Right again. I'd known that too, I'd stressed about it, and I'd still stepped onto this battlefield. There was no way I could just back down after that.

"……!"

Spotting Siesta's legs from below the bus, I burst out from under the vehicle, drew and leveled my second gun, and fired. But…

"…I seriously almost died."

As if she'd predicted my move, Siesta had also fired, and the bullet had zipped right past my head. No, maybe it had grazed it for a few millimeters—a small trickle of blood ran down my cheek.

"Do you want to die?" Siesta tilted her head in a show of innocence.

Still cool as a cucumber, huh? In that case… "Well, you said so yourself—this is war."

Without hesitating or really aiming, I fired a series of shots at Siesta. I wasn't planning to kill her, of course; that would have defeated the whole purpose of this fight. My attacks were based in my trust that *Siesta would evade.* But if even one of those shots managed to graze her, the way hers had against my cheek—

"I see."

Siesta dodged the rain of bullets using moves that would have done an action-movie star proud. Then she took a leap so high, you'd think she launched herself with a trampoline, landing on top of a mound of rubble that was several meters tall. She looked down at me, her face expressionless.

*"Are there tranquilizers in those bullets of yours?"*

She'd seen right through my plan.

"……!"

"Your expression is always so easy to read." With a laid-back suggestion that I should work on my poker face, Siesta evaded another of my bullets by jumping down. "Your conditions for victory don't include killing me. You're only trying to temporarily immobilize me."

...Had she picked up on my scheme when I got impatient and fired at random? Still... "Yeah, all the weapons I'm using have that drug in them. Even 0.01 milligram of this stuff will stop an African elephant or a blue whale. In other words, *if even one shot grazes you, I win.*"

Forget lethal injury: She couldn't even afford to get a scratch. On a battlefield, that restriction would inflict the greatest pressure imaginable. She may have read my hand, but I could use that against her.

"I never planned to let any of your attacks touch me in the first place."

In the next moment, I felt a human presence right behind me. By the time I realized it was Siesta, she'd already kicked my right arm up again, knocking my gun far away.

"...! Look what you did! We're just getting started, and now my right arm's out of commission." With my left hand, I promptly pulled a knife out of my jacket and pointed it at her.

"Is the tip of that coated with the tranquilizer, too?"

Siesta's fist flew at my face; she was holding a ballpoint pen. I knocked it away with the knife, but this time she landed a powerful roundhouse kick to my side.

"...! ...Hff." She'd knocked the wind out of me, and I rolled across the asphalt according to the laws of physics. Needless to say, my entire body hurt. But that pain was no match for my stubborn refusal to quit. I reached for the gun I'd dropped—

"Annnd you're dead."

At the same time... No, Siesta had leveled her gun a moment faster than I had, and she spoke from above me, stopping me. When I slowly raised my head, Siesta had her gun trained on me. She was holding it in her left hand.

"If I pull this trigger now, you'll die. *But I won't do it.* I don't think you're that dumb to not understand what that means, Kimi."

Slowly, Siesta narrowed her blue eyes. Just as I'd begun this fight based on that hijacking incident, Siesta was trying to make me admit I'd lost by re-creating the way she'd pinned Bat down.

"...You call me stupid all the time, but you're ending with that?"

It was like she said, though: If I didn't want to get hurt, if I didn't want to end up with a lethal injury, I needed to back down here. But Siesta was holding that gun in her left hand, and as I gazed at her, a conversation we'd once had came to mind.

It had been an ordinary day. As usual, we were broke, and we were sitting at the dinner table in a cheap apartment in some foreign country. Like the majority of Japanese people, Siesta was poking at the side dishes with chopsticks she held in her right hand, and I'd asked her, "Siesta, weren't you left-handed?"

It was pretty late for that question, and she'd looked perplexed. Well, sure. She ate her meals like that all the time, and when she fought, she held her gun in her right hand. Even so, I'd gotten the impression that she was left-handed because that was the hand she'd used to pull me into this world.

"Let's go on a journey," she'd said. She always held her left hand out to me, smiling that hundred-million-watt smile. That's why I'd gotten the wrong idea.

"Are you stupid, Kimi?" Siesta had said, the way she always did. "I hold my gun in my right hand."

"I think you were trying for *chopsticks* there."

After we'd lobbed jokes at each other, for some reason, Siesta had smiled. "That's why my left hand is the only one I'll ever hold out to you."

It was Siesta's philosophy; I sort of got it and sort of didn't. If I tried to explain it, I would probably reduce it to something trite. As long as I kept the answer hidden inside myself, though, I'd be able to keep taking the left hand she held out to me. So, on that day, I hadn't asked her to elaborate.

If there was just one thing I understood now, it was that Siesta was standing here with a gun in the hand she should have been holding out to me. To borrow her words: I was no longer too dumb to understand what that meant.

"...Yeah, you're right. I lose."

On my knees, with Siesta holding me at gunpoint, I pathetically admitted defeat.

—But...

"So can I say one last thing?"

In the center of a clear, obstacle-free scramble intersection, raising both hands to show I was done resisting, I slowly got to my feet.

"Begging for your life?"

"Don't go killing me after I've admitted I lost."

I glanced at Siesta's eyes; they still looked dangerous. I sighed. "No, that's not it. I just realized you'd asked why I was trying to stop you, and I hadn't told you."

It was the question Siesta had asked right before we'd launched into this fight. Why wouldn't I let her die if she was going to turn into a monster someday? Why did I follow her so persistently, trying to stay involved? In my head, the answer was far too obvious, but I hadn't put it into words for Siesta.

Now that I thought about it, we'd always been like that. We never told each other the important stuff; we'd both assumed the other knew, and we'd always ended up just missing each other. We'd believed in our invisible bond—no, we'd definitely had one of those. It was just that, somewhere along the way, we'd started to rely on it too much.

We'd never confirmed our bond in words, though. We'd thought we didn't need to. We'd figured that when we stood back-to-back in the middle of a firefight, the other person would just get it.

"Thoughts transcend words. When you put it that way, yeah, it sounds good."

Without flinching from the gun that was trained on me, I took one step toward Siesta, then another.

"—What are you...?" Siesta couldn't tell what I was trying to do. She tightened her grip on the gun.

"I figured I'd demonstrate that you need words to properly convey some things."

We'd had three whole years. We'd done all that bantering.

Yet we'd somehow skipped this sort of thing a little too often.

"Why did I want to bring you back to life? Why did I think those three years of constant trouble were fun? You know there's only one answer to that."

They were such simple words, and yet I'd never said them. Saying them out loud would've sounded cliché, at least to me.

"It's because I love you."

When I said that, Siesta's blue eyes widened.

I wasn't going to explain whether that "love" was romantic love or family love or neighborly love. I hadn't managed to put a name to it yet, either. Even so, this feeling had been with me all through those three years without changing a bit, and that was the plainest, clearest term for it.

"That's... What do I even say? I didn't expect that."

Siesta had lowered her gun, although she probably didn't realize it. She sounded rather dazed.

"You went all this time without noticing a thing like that? The Ace Detective herself?"

"...The problem is that your *tsundere* behavior is beyond normal."

We joked around with each other, and then we both smiled a little.

My words really had gotten through to her that time.

"—Except..." But just then, blue flames flickered in Siesta's eyes again. "Some problems can't be overcome with feelings alone."

A gunshot rang out. The bullet whizzed right past my cheek.

"You knew that, too. Getting a romantic confession from you won't be enough to persuade me now."

"I don't recall confessing that."

"Oh, I see. So you were proposing?"

Why were those my only options? Smiling halfheartedly, I obediently put my hands up again. I'd already admitted defeat. My weapons weren't nearby, so I couldn't afford to resist anyway.

"I knew I'd be no match for you."

That was something I'd known right from the start—And so...

"From here on out, *we'll* take you on."

The next instant, there was an earsplitting explosion, and black smoke rose.

"—! A grenade!"

Registering an intruder, Siesta took a huge leap backward to create some distance.

However, a girl interrupted our battle, cutting through the smoke in pursuit of Siesta.

"Not even meeting your maid one last time, after all the trouble you've caused her? That's rather heartless, don't you think?"

The maid revolted against her mistress, holding a rapier. A gust of wind ruffled her pale silver hair. Then—

"*Charlie! Now!*"

From the phone in my breast pocket, a girl's voice echoed across the battlefield. Then I heard a gunshot. It was the sound of a lone agent sniping the Ace Detective from a distant rooftop.

"......! So that's...what it was."

At the last second, Siesta managed to dodge the tranquilizer bullet, and it took a divot out of the asphalt instead. However, she'd caught on to my—or rather, our—plan, and she grimaced.

"Sorry, Siesta. The real final showdown starts now."

Until we saved the Ace Detective, we would never stop.

### ◆ A certain boy's recollection

"Why are you so bad at being a team player?"

The sun was almost set, and Siesta stalked down the lane ahead of me, sighing. In terms of walking speed, neither of us was accommodating the other...but that probably wasn't what she meant.

We were on our way home after safely *failing* a certain mission. It had failed for one clear reason: my hopeless inability to get along with Charlotte Arisaka Anderson, who'd joined us for the maneuver. No matter how often we got scolded for making the same mistake, there was no hope for improvement until the cause was removed.

"I've never teamed up with anybody before, ever. You can ask me to match somebody's pace now, but that hurdle's too high."

Siesta and I had set off on our travels around the world about a year ago. Even before that—I should probably say *unfortunately*—I hadn't had a single person I could call a friend. It was due to my annoying, innate predisposition for getting dragged into trouble. People wanted to avoid it, so they ended up avoiding me. Before I knew it, fifteen years had passed.

"Are you all right with that?"

"What I want has nothing to do with it," I said flatly. I'd thought about trying to change several times, though. Even at fifteen, I sometimes sighed and wondered whether there wasn't a slightly better way to live. Still, as long as I had this predisposition, I wouldn't be able to team up with anyone, and nobody would be able to match my pace.

"Well, I'm used to it." Forcing a smile, I walked over the asphalt. Forget friends, I'd never even had parents. That meant I'd had the skills it took to live alone from the time I was a kid.

"There are some things you can't deal with on your own, though. Like today, for example."

Over her shoulder, Siesta seemed to be implying that I should make some friends. Because I hadn't been able to get along with Charlie today, I'd come close to taking an enemy bullet. Even so, Siesta had ultimately stepped in and rescued me.

"I may not always be around, you know."

...The woman had dragged me on this journey, and now she was making irresponsible comments out of nowhere.

"That said, if I find companions, I might end up putting them in danger instead."

Considering my knack for attracting trouble, the possibility was pretty high. Those were the stars Kimihiko Kimizuka had been born under. Rather than saying I'd resigned myself to that fate, I'd reached enlightenment instead. I didn't need friends who'd walk with me.

"Where are you going?"

The next thing I knew, I heard Siesta's voice behind me.

"Are you stupid, Kimi?"

Then it came up beside me, on my left.

"That's how easy it is to walk with somebody."

The setting sun dyed the pavement orange, and two black shadows stretched across it.

"Of course I'm not your lover, and I'm sure I'm not even your friend. I don't even know whether you could call me a companion. But..." Siesta faced forward as she spoke. "Right now, I'm standing next to you."

The orange light shone gently on her pale silver hair. When I stole a glance at her profile, it seemed more dignified and beautiful than any famous painting or sculpture.

"You'll have comrades too someday." Looking over at me, Siesta gave a soft smile. "And I'm sure you'll combine your strengths to accomplish something."

...I dunno about that. I can't really picture it. Then there was that predisposition of mine. Even if Siesta was right, those future comrades might all be weirdos.

"Well, if it ever happens, I'll introduce you."

"Yes, I'll be looking forward to it."

Treading on our long shadows, we started down the sunset lane, side by side.

## ◆ A blank shot of an oath, told at ten thousand meters

The grenade had shrouded the battlefield in thick black smoke. A lone girl leaped through it, her maid uniform fluttering in the wind.

"We're counting on you, Noches."

Holding my useless right arm, I slipped into the shadow of some rubble.

"I see. So these are your companions now."

Just before I made it, though—for just a moment, Siesta's blue eyes found me through a gap in the windblown smoke.

The wish to stop her from dying *belonged to all of us*. If you defined *companions* as people who shared a common goal, then the girl who was sprinting with a sword in one hand definitely counted.

"Still, I never dreamed you'd rebel against me."

Siesta leveled her gun at Noches, preparing to fight back…but the weapon flew out of her hand, sniped from a distance.

"Charlotte, Yui. You too?"

Siesta glanced at a building in the direction from the bullet but promptly returned her gaze to her immediate opponent. "Noches. I don't believe you were made for combat," she grumbled at her former maid, dodging a one-handed sword thrust.

"Mm, yes. I anticipated this situation and bluffed."

"You're telling me you laid the groundwork two full weeks ago to make me let my guard down? Those are some extremely thorough preparations."

Siesta's response was cool; she probably hadn't taken Noches seriously. Had she realized we'd borrowed the power of a certain Inventor again?

"My former mistress taught me to prepare to resolve an incident before it occurred, you see." Noches crouched down, then closed the distance between them in a rush.

"Is that sword coated with tranquilizer as well?"

It was. If it so much as grazed Siesta, we'd win this fight on the spot.

"…! I may be an android, but I think you're more overpowered than I am, Mistress."

Siesta had pulled out that ballpoint pen again and used it to knock the sword out of Noches's hand.

"Oh? They do say the pen is mightier than the sword, though."

"…You've got a comeback for everything, don't you?"

At that, Noches drew a pair of pistols. Firing two shots in a magnificent display of ambidexterity, she nailed her earthbound target… Or she would have if the target had been anybody else.

"—Not one of your attacks will ever work on me."

Launching herself off the ground, Siesta flung herself backward as if she were performing a Fosbury flop. The bullets cut through space beneath her.

"Then we'll just keep going until one does."

Noches kept up a barrage of bullets as if our lives depended on it. She took an endless series of heavy weaponry out of her maid uniform. As I took in the situation, I thought about what I should be doing, then attempted to relocate.

"An endurance contest? That's not very smart."

Meanwhile, Siesta kept evading Noches's bullets with peerless accuracy. She jumped up from the asphalt, ran across walls of buildings, sprinted over roofs, leaped into empty space, and finally reached the elevated train tracks. The primordial seed's attack had left them thickly covered with vines, and no trains ran on the deserted rails.

"I won't let you escape."

Noches went after Siesta, bounding off of abandoned cars and telephone poles as footholds.

"...They're completely ignoring me."

That was convenient, though. I couldn't take the shortest possible route to the tracks the way they were doing. I ran through the empty, ruined city for several minutes, finally managing to make it to the station.

I jumped the unmanned ticket gate, dashed up the stairs without pausing for breath, then sprinted all the way to the end of the platform, stumbling as I went. Then I gazed down the tracks with misty eyes—and saw Noches, down on one knee; Siesta had her at gunpoint. She must have taken her guns, and she had Noches pinned.

"*Charlie! The wind died!*"

Just then—the voice of a certain idol filtered onto the battlefield from the wireless earphone Noches had happened to drop. A bullet fired from nowhere in particular skimmed past, below Siesta.

The sniper had fired from a building several hundred meters away. With Saikawa's left eye reading the wind currents for her, Charlotte Arisaka Anderson's sniping was even more accurate.

True, Seed had retrieved Saikawa's seed, but the ability that dwelled in her left eye had remained. It was as if Seed had been trying to leave that sapphire eye in this world on its own.

Now, if only the pressure of their combo attack slowed Siesta down—

"—That's twice. That attack won't work, either."

But my hopes were immediately shattered. First, Siesta kicked Noches out of her way. Then she turned back, pointing her gun at *the blond agent who'd been sneaking up on her from behind.*

"...Ma'am. You weren't surprised." Charlie froze. She was holding a dagger at the ready.

Since Charlie had been sniping from a distant building, there was no way Siesta could have anticipated that she'd climb up onto the tracks. However—"I knew my assistant and Noches *were letting me hear Yui's voice on purpose.* The instructions she was giving you were a bluff. You were actually lurking nearby the whole time, waiting for a chance."

—She'd caught on.

Staring down the barrel of the gun, Charlie bit her lip and tossed her knife away.

"I never thought you'd turn on me too, Charlie."

"Apprentices always surpass their masters eventually."

Just then, another gunshot echoed, and a bullet skimmed beneath Siesta.

"I'm impressed she can do all that with only her left eye as a guide."

The bullet struck the rails with a fierce metallic clang, momentarily diverting Siesta's attention. Charlie grabbed the chance to back up, putting some distance between them. Then she drew her gun and pointed it at Siesta.

"You thought you could beat me with a quick draw?" Siesta extended her right arm too, aiming her own gun at Charlie.

"...You're right. I might not be able to beat you yet, Ma'am. But..." Charlie's voice grew stronger. "Maybe *we* can."

That was the signal.

"Why did I get this job when I don't have a license?"

Straddling the bike we'd prepared, I shook my head and cranked the accelerator. As the engine roared, I jumped down from the platform onto the tracks. And then...

"...! Why do you have that, Kimi?"

Charlie threw herself off the tracks. In her place, I charged at Siesta, holding the Ace Detective's musket at the ready.

"...I don't believe I gave that to you."

"Nope. I'm just here to give it back."

*Ever since that day four years ago, as your assistant, it's been my job to give this to you.*

"But first..." My target was twenty meters away. Steering the bike with my knees, I held the musket with both hands and fired.

"I see. I really wasn't expecting that one. ...Still." Siesta's blue eyes turned toward me as I drove down the deserted tracks on the motorcycle.

"—That's three. I believed you'd team up."

Siesta pulled the trigger of the gun in her left hand. The shot was so accurate, it could have passed through the eye of a needle; the bullets we'd fired collided in midair with a bang, canceling each other out.

By the time it happened, though, my motorcycle was right in front of Siesta. If I used the momentum to crash into her...

"...Dammit!"

Yanking the handlebars to the side, I threw my weight to the right in an attempt to avoid the collision. Of course, I was flung off into empty space—

"Are you stupid, Kimi?"

I felt as if I'd heard a voice scolding me for being reckless. Then, for just a moment, my body seemed to pause, hovering lightly in midair.

"...Owww."

Right after that, though, I rolled onto the tracks. I felt as if I'd gotten a full-body lashing with a whip. But there was no time to groan in pain or catch my breath. Lifting my face from the gravel, I checked on the situation—and what I saw was...

"This is a battlefield, Charlotte."

"———!"

Siesta's bullet grazed Charlie's right shoulder. That shot was probably an indispensable courtesy for an agent who risked her life in battle.

"...Not yet. Ma'am...I still..." Charlie got back up. Her shoulder was bleeding, yet she still gripped her gun, trying to correct her teacher's error. As Siesta looked at her apprentice, for just a moment, the muzzle of her gun seemed to waver. Was she thinking of where she should shoot in order to be sure she'd immobilized her target, or—

"…! Charlie!" Just then, a girl's shadow appeared. The voice belonged to a certain idol, the one I'd been hearing over the phone a moment ago. Right now, I was hearing the real thing from ten meters away.

Siesta sighed, then murmured, "—Fourth time. I knew about that dedication, too."

She must have been paying attention to the intervals between the gunshots and the impacts and realized the sniper was gradually coming closer. Saikawa stepped in front of Charlie, gun in hand. Siesta pointed her own gun at her.

"I won't let you."

Just then, Noches slipped in like the wind and kicked Siesta's right hand up. Her gun flew high in the air.

"Sorry, but your timing is perfect."

Instead of flinching back, Siesta landed a precise kick to Noches's abdomen.

"——!"

Someone shrieked, but I couldn't tell who. Noches went flying. She collided with Saikawa and Charlie, taking them out with her, and all three of them rolled onto the gravel ballast between the rails. Finally, no one was blocking Siesta's way.

"Are we done now?"

Siesta closed her eyes, taking slow, deep breaths. When plenty of time passed, she opened her eyes again. I couldn't read any emotion in them. The Ace Detective was her usual self.

"Nagisa is still asleep; she can't come here. In that case, who's next? The Oracle or the Assassin…? The Vampire? Well, it doesn't matter who it is; I won't lose."

Using her left hand, Siesta picked up the musket I'd dropped onto the rails, then loudly fired it into the sky.

"To protect the world, I will kill myself. To achieve that, I will defeat you. By defeating you, I can protect you. This is my final job as the Ace Detective."

Siesta was a Tuner, one of the guardians of the world, and this was a hero's oath. A seed that could destroy the world lay asleep inside her. To keep it from sprouting, she would end her story with her own hands.

"And so you are my final enemy—Kimihiko Kimizuka."

Siesta pointed her musket at me. I was back on my feet.

"Geez. You say my actual name for the first time ever, and it's in a situation like this?" Smiling with chagrin, I trained my own gun on Siesta.

Still, for the flawless ace detective, this was unusual—that oath of hers needed two corrections. The first was...

"...Your companions never learn, do they?"

Three figures had gotten to their feet behind me, and Siesta sighed.

It wasn't just me. Nobody here had given up on standing in her way. She'd also gotten one other thing wrong.

"Siesta, we won't let you complete that final job."

I'd already seen a way to win this.

## ◇ A certain girl's recollection

"And? What sort of partner do you think you could make it work with?" I asked my assistant.

We were sipping black tea in an open-air terrace café. That day, he'd messed up during a certain mission, and we'd held a postmortem session about it on the way home. In fact, we weren't finished yet. I went on, turning the conversation his way, hoping to convince him to make some friends.

"What type of person could I get along with...?" Across the table from me, my assistant mulled it over, unexpectedly serious. "A kind, big-sister type who can tolerantly embrace all my flaws," he answered finally.

"You're talking about your taste in girls, not a companion." Honestly. And here I was attempting to have a serious conversation. "Not only that, but you just described me to a tee."

"How, exactly? You're the polar opposite of that."

I hadn't been playing dumb, but he hit me with a comeback anyway. I don't understand this boy.

"You keep focusing on me, but what about you, Siesta?" he asked. "Do you have any companions?"

Several faces rose in my mind, including Charlie's, of course. The Oracle in her high clock tower, for example. The red-haired police officer—or was she more of a comrade than a friend?

In addition…I had the feeling there had been others. I'd definitely had people I could call companions, long ago. My memory of them was oddly hazy, though, as if someone had sealed it… I knew they'd been there, but I could no longer recall the girls' names or their faces.

"…Maybe that's why I keep pestering you about them."

Because I'd lost mine. In exchange, I wanted my assistant to have them.

"I don't get what you mean by 'friend' or 'companion' in the first place." My assistant didn't seem to have heard me. He was sounding like a middle schooler with delusions of omnipotence. Although at his age, he technically should have been attending middle school.

"You put the other person first sometimes… You want to. I think that sort of relationship counts as 'friends' or 'companions,' don't you?"

There were no clear standards, of course. Still, I felt it was necessary to attempt to put formless concepts into words once in a while.

"Isn't that what we are, then?"

I hadn't been expecting that remark, and my hand froze partway to my teacup.

"…When I couldn't make it work with Charlie today and almost got myself shot, you put yourself on the line to protect me. That means you think of me as, uh… I mean, you know…"

My assistant's eyes went to my bandaged left shoulder; his expression was a complicated mix of emotions. Even though, to me, a wound of this level was nothing to write home about.

"I protected you because of our contract."

It was a promise I'd made to my assistant a year ago. I'd told him I would protect him. I'd taken him on this journey on that condition. That meant it was simply my job to put myself on the line when he was in danger…

"For all that, you looked pretty panicked today." For some reason, my assistant was gazing me, as if he'd stumbled onto something entertaining. "Actually, Siesta, you tend to get pretty rattled when I'm really in trouble."

"_____!"

*He's awfully impertinent for an assistant. I just—I only—*

"Haah…"

I couldn't work up the energy to respond. Instead, I heaved a rather weighty sigh. The important thing to me was protecting my clients' interests. As long as I could do that, I was satisfied.

"Come to think of it, Kimi, you didn't order coffee. That's unusual."

Suddenly curious—eager to change the subject, really—I pointed this out to my assistant. He generally did order hot coffee, but this time he was drinking tea, like me.

"It's just a black tea kinda day."

"—I see."

We sat on the terrace, sipping the same tea and gazing at the same setting sun.

## ◇ That's how I define "living"

"Siesta, we won't let you complete that final job."

On top of the long elevated track, my assistant pointed his gun at me. Taking a cue from him, the other three surrounded me. The four of them formed a hollow square, positioning themselves at diagonals to each other, apparently determined not to let me get away.

"…Are you people stupid?"

*If you do this, even if you get your wish, the seed will eat away at me until I become a monster. There's no stopping that.*

"Can't you understand that disappearing is the last job I'm capable of?"

My final duty. To tell the truth, this should have been over and done with long ago. Last year, to be exact: when I'd died in order to seal Hel. I'd entrusted my last wish to my assistant, Nagisa, Yui, and Charlie. Through

Noches, I'd set them free of the problems and curses that bound them. Once that was done, my job should have been complete.

But my assistant and Nagisa had overruled the future I'd visualized. The result had been several kinds of chaos, and Nagisa had fallen victim to the distortion. And yet, although I'd meant to seal Hel as my final job, she had defeated the primordial seed and ended the story in a new way.

That meant the fact that I was still here was just an extension of that battle. It was redundant. This was an epilogue that had never needed to be written. ...Even so. I was on this battlefield, I had taken up this gun again, and so...

"I will never abandon my job. I'll lay my life on the line and fulfill the duty of the Ace Detective."

Several gunshots echoed, and the final battle began in earnest.

"—I was already sick of seeing bullets about four years ago."

Bullets flew at me from four directions, but if one grasps the angle of the muzzle down to the millimeter, it's possible to be faster than a gun. The bullets ended up striking the gravel ballast or nothing at all, and I ran with the wind to leave them behind.

I was up against four enemies, but they were all injured already. If I picked them off one by one, they wouldn't be a problem. First, my apologies, but—

"Yui Saikawa. Your left eye is trouble."

"......!"

That eye's kinetic vision was far beyond what ordinary humans could achieve. In combat, it was bound to be more useful than any heavy weaponry. Planning to take that power away from them, I ran up to Yui. She looked startled.

I had no intention of killing her, of course, or of damaging that blue eye. My assistant had brought the musket I was holding. That meant it was most likely loaded with tranquilizer bullets. ...No, he might have assumed that I'd steal the gun, in which case it was possible that only the first bullet was a tranquilizer. I'd just have to test it. I'd graze Yui with a bullet, and if all went well, she'd sleep for a little while. Rapidly coming to that conclusion, I began to squeeze the trigger—

"——!"

Right then, Charlie took cover behind Yui. At this angle, I'd shoot her—and I'd hit her in the head. The shoulder would have been acceptable, but a head wound could end up being fatal.

"...That's not like you at all, Charlie."

Grumbling over my apprentice's bad judgment call, I temporarily lowered my weapon and put some distance between us.

"Mistress Siesta. This is a battlefield. We deal in lives here, correct?"

Suddenly, I sensed someone coming in for a fatal blow. I twisted away, and Noches's sword swept through the spot where I'd been standing a moment earlier. The blade was coated with tranquilizer; if it grazed me, I'd be finished. The sheer number of restrictions was maddening, and I brought my gun to bear on her. Her body was mechanical, and with a few exceptions, she'd be fine no matter where I shot her. So this time, I relaxed and—

"Noches!"

As if to shield the maid, my assistant darted out in front of her.

"...! Are you stupid, Kimi?!"

At the very last second, I fired into empty space. There was no telling what my assistant might do, and if I hit him in the wrong place, I could kill him.

"Your instincts are as bad as ever, Kimi."

In terms of recent events, I remembered his battle with Chameleon on the cruise ship. He'd put himself in the wrong place that time too and had ended up taking the enemy's attack. No matter how you looked at it, I—or in this case, Noches—was better at absorbing enemy attacks than he was, and yet—

"...Is that what this is?"

Just then, a terrible hunch ran through my mind. At the same time, a bullet streaked right past my face.

"I'm sorry, Charlie. Siesta seems to have caught on more quickly than we expected."

"Well, she is the first and only teacher I decided to respect until I died."

A few meters ahead, Charlie was smiling proudly. She pointed her gun at me again.

"If you don't dodge, I'll hit you."

It was immediately clear that she wasn't talking to me.

"Yeah. It'll probably be okay, though."

"_____!"

*Bang!* My assistant was standing behind me. Just as the gunshot rang out, I grabbed his shirtfront, and we fell together, evading Charlie's bullet.

"Because Siesta's going to save me. See?"

Flat on the ground, my assistant broke into a smile. Then he sat up and pointed his gun at me.

"Is every last one of you that stupid...?!" I whirled around, scanning my four enemies. "So this is your final ploy for cornering me?"

If I tried to attack one of them, someone else would step in to shield them. Yet they'd pull their triggers with no hesitation, even if there was a risk of hitting one of their companions. It was a foolish plan, riddled with contradictions. Did they want to protect each other, or was stopping me their top priority? At a glance, I couldn't tell which it was. However, if there was an answer that would resolve those inconsistencies—

"Yeah, Siesta. *There's absolutely no way you can kill us.*"

The next moment, Noches's bullet bore down on me...and on my assistant behind me.

"...!"

Sweeping my musket to the side, I knocked it away. Meanwhile, Yui took aim at Charlie, who was on my other side.

"I told you—!"

There wasn't even time to talk. As Yui fired, I pressed my trigger as well; our shots collided in midair, and the one that was headed for Charlie was knocked off course.

Although I'd said this was a war, I'd been maneuvering around so that the others wouldn't die. Sooner or later, the countless bullets that were flying every which way would mortally wound them. I'd been instinctively avoiding that outcome. However, the four of them were taking advantage of my hesitation by intentionally putting themselves in danger, trying to confuse me and restrict my movements.

"You were particularly hesitant when you attacked Saikawa, who's not used to fighting, and when I almost passed out on the motorcycle, you saved me on reflex. You're a softie. Not being able to kill your companions is your strength and your one weakness."

...The old me wouldn't have hesitated at a time like this. I'd prioritized executing my duties, believing I'd bring about happiness for the greatest number of people that way. As a matter of fact, I was confident that doing so had protected many of my clients' interests.

As a result, the old me had considered that sort of hesitation self-indulgence. And yet as far as one person was concerned, it was kindness, and to another, it even counted as passion. Before I knew it, I'd learned these things. That hesitation was the reason my heart was still pounding. At this point, it was part of my heart itself.

"...What a cowardly move. Don't you think you're treating your lives too lightly?"

"First of all, Ma'am, your life is riding on this battle. It would be rude of us not to stake ours," Charlie declared bravely. She sounded like a true agent. Operating on the same logic, I'd shot her in the shoulder once, and I couldn't think of a response for her. In that case, what I needed to do now was—

"I won't let you get away!"

Yui's left eye had seen what I was about to do. Just as I was about to jump off the elevated track—a loud boom distracted me. The ground under my feet shook violently. Then, with a sustained rumble, it crumbled away.

"......! Explosives."

Had Noches set them up? I didn't have time to check, and there would have been no point anyway. The elevated track I'd been standing on a moment ago had turned into rubble, and I was tossed into the air, joining a rain of gravel and scrap iron.

"_____!"

The free fall lasted for about ten meters. There were no obstacles; if I'd been prepared to jump, I could have landed without trouble. I'd been caught by surprise, though, and I'd also been swallowed up in an avalanche of gravel. While I did manage to make the safest possible landing, I banged myself up royally on the asphalt.

The strategy they'd put together must have been based on trust that I'd survive something like this. ...But even if I was spared, they'd be—

"...Assistant!"

"I swear... You never think about yourself first."

I aimed my musket toward the voice and saw my assistant standing beyond the clouds of dust, a gun in his left hand. By this point, I lost count of how many times I'd seen this configuration. Behind him, the other three climbed out of the rubble. I guessed Noches had protected my assistant, while Charlie had kept Yui safe.

"Haah...! You look...awful..."

My assistant's right arm hung limply, and he was bleeding from his head. The black jacket he was so proud of was all ragged.

"...Haah... So...do you."

Didn't he know there were things you should never say to a girl? Honestly!

"...! ......Haah."

I couldn't hide my rough breathing or my heart rate, though.

The worst part was that I'd sprained my leg. Now I wouldn't be able to make a clean escape either way.

"...Why did it end up like this?"

It shouldn't have been this way. Why did my assistant and I have to hold each other at gunpoint in the first place? This story should have ended when the primordial seed was sealed. But I didn't want Nagisa to remain unconscious, and I'd decided to watch the story just a little longer. To see it until the end of my assistant's Route X.

I'd boarded a plane with him for what I'd decided would be the last time. We'd traveled overseas, got caught up in an unexpected incident, and encountered a new enemy. My assistant considered the fight with the Phantom Thief an extension of the primordial seed crisis. Therefore, I would remain the detective, Kimihiko Kimizuka would remain my assistant, and the two of us would continue to fight the world's enemies, Phantom Thief included… If I'd said I hadn't imagined that future for even a moment, I would have been lying.

However, I'd been right the first time: I couldn't go any further than this. I couldn't spend forever soaking in that tepid epilogue. I would simply carry out my role as a player on Route X, in my position as the Ace Detective. Technically, I should have died a year ago. The fact that I'd been involved in this at all was a miracle in and of itself.

And so, now I confronted Kimihiko Kimizuka, my final enemy—no, the protagonist. I had no intention of losing. Of course I didn't. Losing would mean *that I'd be saved by the protagonist.* I couldn't allow such a lukewarm story to play out this way.

"You are justice, and I'm evil. That's fine. It's what I've always wanted."

Using just my good leg, I launched myself off the ground. This battle would be over soon. Gun in hand, I raced toward my last opponent.

"Kimizuka, go right!"

That was Yui's voice. Following her instructions from a distance, my assistant flung himself to the side, evading my bullet.

"…! Are you seriously okay with that?!" Even as he rolled on the ground, he fired at me. I dodged, moving only my upper body. "Siesta, tell me. What's your wish?"

I heard more gunshots, this time from Noches and Charlie, far behind me. If they so much as grazed me, I'd lose.

"I only have one wish: I want you to live. All of you."

That was why I turned my long-barreled gun on the girls: to fire the bullets that would let them live.

"That can't be it!"

——! Stubborn. My assistant had blocked my path again, and my hands started to tremble slightly. My heart pounded loudly, and my shallow breathing made my vision go hazy.

"—How would you know?!"

"You said so yourself!" he shouted. The grief in his expression was intense. He said it had happened a year ago, after the fight with Hel, when the pollen had put him to sleep. The comment must have slipped out just before my consciousness vanished. A wisp of thought I'd never meant for him to hear.

"I don't remember anything of the sort," I told him, firing to shake off my hesitation. I hadn't taken aim, and I missed him by a mile. I'd strengthened my resolve, though. Evading the bullets Charlie and the others fired from far away, I began my final shootout with my assistant.

"What, you're saying you don't remember something you said yourself?" He couldn't possibly have time for idle chatter, but as he fired, he kept talking. "If you won't say it, I will."

............

"You don't want to die, do you?"
Impossible. A wish like that, *now of all times?*

"We'll figure it out somehow."
*You can't.*

"I'll find a way to let you live!"
*Listen, I told you that's not possible.*

"You always wished happiness for your clients, and those clients are all the people on this planet. How could you be the only one who doesn't count? That can't be right!"
*You're wrong. I was happy.*
I was quite content—or I should have been.
And yet...
"Siesta, I want you to live."
*If you say a thing like that to me, I'll—*
"——!"

My assistant fired at my left arm; it was a shot meant to keep me alive. On reflex, I moved my arm, sweeping my musket sideways and knocking the bullet out of the air. ...Even so, my contradictory thoughts asked my mind the same question.

*What is your real wish?*

"—I..."

I asked myself one more time. I'd already died once. There was no need to keep up appearances; I didn't need pride. I'd throw away shame and my reputation, get rid of all calculations and deception.

For now, I'd forget my role and the position I was in, pretend my history and the things I'd said had never happened. There was no point in thinking about some nebulous future. Just for now, I'd pretend not to see my responsibility toward this world.

Say I was the only one who existed here, in this moment. What would I wish for? What dream would I want to come true? Right now, it didn't matter whether it was possible or impossible. This wasn't about whether it was reckless or unachievable. If there was just one thing I wanted—

The answer was simple.

"—I want to drink tea with you again."

I wanted to live.

"Right. Wish accepted."

My assistant pointed his gun at my face.

*I see. So that's the way you smile now.*

"You talk like a detective," I responded lightly.

If I did nothing, his shot would just barely graze my cheek.

If it did, I'd get my wish.

My dearest partner, the protagonist, would save me.

That had to be the happy ending everyone was hoping for.

With the bullet that would end everything right in front of me, I told him:

"But a detective mustn't lose to her assistant."

I'd never show him my back.

It wasn't right to let the assistant see his detective admit defeat.

I dodged the bullet, then turned the musket I'd had for my whole life as the Ace Detective on him.

"Yeah, that's right. I really am no match for you. That's why..."

My assistant's lips moved.

"She's going to take over that wish of yours for me, Siesta."

In the next moment, sensing someone behind me, I turned and readied my musket.

"...Why are you here?"

My eyes widened.

"—As the queen of the land of the dead, I forbid you to come to this world."

I was facing a girl with short black hair, dressed in a military uniform.

"Why are you...? Hel?"

The next moment...

The girl in the uniform threw her arms around me, hugging me tightly.

"Tricked you. I'm sorry. It's me, Nagisa."

## ◇ Buenas noches

"Wh-why...?" I murmured.

However, I'd actually anticipated that Nagisa would come here.

I'd borrowed her body once, awakening in order to help my assistant. In the same way, if it was for his sake, Nagisa would come running no matter where he was. People might call it "improbably convenient" and laugh, but *that was how we were wired.*

"It's been a long time, Siesta."

Her arms gently released their hold on me.

Nagisa's soft smile was right in front of me. She'd chopped off her long hair.

She got me good. Who'd have thought she'd appear disguised as Hel?

"You haven't changed, Nagisa," I commented, a bit spitefully. I was somewhat chagrined that she'd outfoxed me.

"Really? I think I changed my look pretty drastically."

"I meant on the inside. And what is this anyway? Did you get your heart broken or something?"

"...I really wish you wouldn't just decide I'm the losing heroine." Nagisa gave me a long look with narrowed eyes, and then we smiled at each other—But...

"...Hm? Huh?"

For some reason, I felt weak all of a sudden, and my knees buckled.

"Whoops!" Nagisa hugged me again, this time to keep me from falling. I didn't recall getting hit with a tranquilizer bullet, but...for some reason, I was suddenly sleepy.

"I'm sorry," Nagisa apologized in a small voice, right in my ear. I really couldn't stay on my feet, and I dropped to my knees, still leaning against her.

"What on earth...?"

Come to think of it, I could feel a tiny prickle of pain on my left upper arm. I forced my heavy eyelids open and examined that spot. There was no blood. When Nagisa had first hugged me, something had—

"—It's a tranquilizer."

That was my assistant's voice.

He came toward us, still in his ragged jacket, leaning on Noches for support. "It's a special drug *a certain underground doctor* compounded for us. I hear it's based on the pollen that put me to sleep."

"...So that's what it was."

The weapons my assistant and the others used must have been covered in it. The Inventor had left us a week ago, but apparently he'd returned. He'd probably heard that Nagisa had awakened and wanted to keep an eye on her progress. Then my assistant had proposed this plan, and he'd helped out.

"But what then? What are you planning to do to me once I'm asleep and unable to resist?" Frustrated that I'd fallen for his scheme, I teased my assistant, resting my head on Nagisa's lap.

"Don't be an idiot. All this time, and still no trust?"

Yes, that's the face I wanted to see.

When I smiled, my assistant sighed and did the same. But then, as he explained their reasons for putting me to sleep, his face grew serious again. "This way, we should be able to temporarily stop the seed in your heart from growing."

*Oh, I knew it.* Closing my eyes, I listened to my assistant. He had a tone that was brusque yet somehow gentle.

"After Natsunagi woke up yesterday, when she and I were brainstorming ways to save you, we picked up on something weird. While you were asleep in Natsunagi's heart, when Chameleon almost killed me, you came to save me just once."

It had happened more than a month ago. On a large cruise ship, I'd borrowed Nagisa's body and fought Chameleon alongside my assistant. Nagisa had talked me into using her body.

"The problem was that 'just once' bit." Sounding rather sad, my assistant explained, "Why did you only wake up that one time? Why didn't you even try...? It was all to avoid activating the seed that had taken root in your heart. Meaning as long as you're asleep, as long as you stay unconscious, that seed won't grow."

He was right.

Had Nagisa been the one who'd realized it? No, it might have been my assistant, since he'd spent the past few days with me. On our trip to New York, I'd slept even longer than I used to. It had been a defensive reaction, an unconscious attempt to protect myself.

"But Assistant...you've also realized there's no point to this, haven't you?"

Opening my heavy eyelids, I saw that Noches, Charlie, and Yui had joined Nagisa and my assistant. They were all watching me, and it was a little embarrassing. ...Still, I understood. These were my assistant's current companions.

*It's all right. He's all right now.*

Relieved, I told him he didn't have to do this. "Putting me to sleep is only a stopgap measure. Besides, there's no guarantee that this will arrest the seed's growth entirely. A few years down the road, the seed that will destroy the world may sprout and turn me into a monster. I may kill all of you someday. And so, really—"

"*We* knew that when *we* chose this." My assistant knelt next to me and continued. "Anyway, Stephen's the one who gave me this tranquilizer. You know what that means, right?"

"...I see. You really don't cut corners anymore, do you?"

The Inventor, Stephen Bluefield, refused to work on hopeless cases. That let him focus his efforts on lives that could still be saved. Since he'd prescribed this drug to me, I must still have a chance. He wouldn't forgive me for giving up on life. After all, I'd been the one to quote his philosophy at him earlier.

"—It looks like I've been utterly defeated."

Detectives must protect their clients' interests and grant their wishes.

Nagisa had made both our wishes—for the other to live—come true at the same time.

That was something the old me hadn't been able to do. I'd only been able to make it happen with my own death. However, Nagisa had once made the same mistake as I had—and then she'd found this answer. She'd definitely beaten me.

"Ma'am! Ma'am...!"

My right hand was warm with tears and another's body heat—Charlie had taken my hand in both of hers, and she couldn't keep from crying any longer. No matter how much time passed, my first apprentice was always adorable.

"...Heh-heh. I see. In the end, you two surpassed me as well."

The drug was really taking hold on me now, and my eyelids grew heavier. Still, pretending to gaze up at the sky, I peeked at my assistant's and Charlie's faces. *Have you two started getting along a little better?* I didn't know, but there was one thing I was sure of.

"You've gotten stronger, haven't you?"

Strong enough to surpass me.

The remark seemed to startle my assistant; his eyes went wide. Then his expression softened. "Yeah, actually, Charlie and I were faking like we didn't get along. All part of the plan. We're actually a great team and best buds. Right?"

"Um, huh? ...Yes, that's right! I—I love Kimizuka!" In response to my assistant's forced setup line, Charlie gave an extremely stiff smile.

"...Heh, heh-heh. I see. That's good."

I'd never dreamed I'd get to see these two with their arms around each other's shoulders, even if it was just an act. I laughed in spite of myself.

"You've got it rough too, Nagisa. All these rivals."

"Aaaaah! Aaaaah! I can't heaaar yooou!"

When I teased her, Nagisa clapped her hands over her ears in an exaggerated gesture... Then, like my assistant, she grinned. "Hey, Siesta?"

"Hm?"

The wind ruffled Nagisa's short hair.

"Thank you for giving me a place to belong, Ace Detective," she said, smiling through her tears. Now that sounded familiar.

"You took the words right out of my mouth." Reaching out with some difficulty, I wiped her tears away with my fingertips. "Thank you for teaching me about emotions, Ace Detective."

Because Nagisa was there... *I'm sure I'm able to smile now, surrounded by this irreplaceable happiness, because of your passion.*

"Siesta." At Yui and Noches's gentle encouragement, my assistant took my left hand.

"Assistant." Squeezing his hand back, I said the words that suddenly came to mind. "If you ever lose your energy, the first thing you need to do is get a lot of sleep."

That seemed to puzzle him; still, as I blinked slowly, he watched me.

There were a few last things I wanted to make sure I told him. I wasn't able to handle complicated thoughts at this point, so I just drew on my recent memories. "And then bathe, all right? Cleanse your body, cleanse your mind. Then eat lots of food."

"...Right, like earlier."

"Don't just eat pizza, though. Try to strike a healthy balance and get moderate exercise. And then… That's right. You have lots of companions, so if you're ever worried about something, talk it over with them right away. You tend to hold everything in."

"Hey, you have no right to tell me that." My assistant geared up to flick my forehead with his middle finger, the way he had earlier—but then he gently brushed my bangs aside with his fingertip. "You're talking about nothing but me again."

"Am I? I'm sleepy. I can't really tell."

However, in terms of regrets, that was about all I had left. As long as my assistant ate plenty of food, and laughed with his friends, *and lived through mediocre, peaceful, extraordinary days*, that was enough for me.

"Haaah. Good grief." From the look in his eyes, he seemed to be testing me. "You really like me far too much, don't you?" he asked, trying to hit me with an extra-large helping of payback.

"Yes, you're right. I like you."

"…Don't just give it to me straight like that."

Mm-hmm. As the Ace Detective, I can't let my assistant have the upper hand. With Nagisa's help, I sat up next to him. He heaved a big sigh, then smiled wryly.

"Are you stupid or what, Siesta?"

My response was obvious.

"Geez. That's not fair."

We both cracked up, and then Nagisa, Charlie, Yui, and Noches were all laughing. Even as tears stained their cheeks.

"Someday, I'll…no, *we'll* wake you up. I swear we will. And so, until then—"

My assistant squeezed my left hand.

"Good night, Ace Detective."

★   ★   ★

That was the last thing my assistant whispered to me, the girl who loved her naps.

A ray of sunlight shone through the thick clouds, illuminating us warmly.

"Yes, I'll be waiting."

Once again, someday.

In the sky, at ten thousand meters.

# Epilogue

A week had passed.

By school standards, summer vacation was long over, and class—which I'd skipped as a matter of course—had begun as usual. As far as the calendar was concerned, it was autumn.

That said, the light that shone through the window was still hot, and the afternoon sun was bright, so I closed the hospital room's thin curtains.

"Hey, are you listening?" said a woman's husky voice from the telephone.

Of course it was the red-haired policewoman, Fuubi Kase. It felt like she'd been calling an awful lot lately. Maybe she'd fallen for me.

"Yeah, I'm listening. You were talking about how the police had a commendation for me, the super high school kid who saved the world."

"That's not even a thing."

No, huh?

"It's about Seed." Sighing in mild disgust, Ms. Fuubi brought up the enemy of the world we'd defeated a few weeks back. "That huge tree where *he's* sleeping really is a bit special."

She was talking about the huge tree that had swallowed the shopping mall in the heart of the city. Earlier, she'd mentioned that the tree where Seed was sealed held atoms that humanity had never encountered before. Apparently that investigation had made some progress.

The subject was way out of my league, though, but the Ace Detective had spent years fighting the primordial seed, so it wasn't unrelated to her. I had a hunch we weren't going to be able to ignore it forever.

"Yggdrasil." Ms. Fuubi pulled a foreign-sounding word out of nowhere.

"What brought that on?"

"It's what they named the tree. Since it's under observation and all." I heard her exhale cigarette smoke on the other end of the line.

Yggdrasil. Also known as the world tree in Scandinavian mythology, the enormous tree was said to encompass nine worlds, one of which was ours. Would humanity end up coexisting with that thing forever? And how would it affect us...?

"Sorry, Ms. Fuubi. My friends will be arriving soon."

That question didn't have a quick or easy answer. Glancing at the clock, I got ready to hang up.

"Ha! Now, there's a word I never thought I'd hear you say."

"Well, people change," I told her, and heard an unusually cheerful sigh in response. "Okay, so, see you around."

"Yeah. Give my regards to the ace detective." Without specifying which one, Ms. Fuubi hung up.

And with perfect timing, the door to the hospital room rattled open. "Siestaaaa! We came to visit you... Oh, you're here too, Kimizuka. I thought you would be."

The girl who came in was Yui Saikawa, the world's cutest idol. With a small smile, she looked from the girl who slept on the bed to me, who was standing beside it.

This was the hospital run by Stephen the Inventor. I'd been here since this morning, visiting Siesta.

"He always is. No matter when I visit, that guy is here, too." The blond girl who'd entered after Saikawa folded her arms and sighed, looking at me. That's weird; after a certain recent situation, I'd assumed we were best buds.

"—Whoops! Whoa. Sorry, you two, lemme through! I'm just going to set this on the side table!"

Nagisa Natsunagi was the last one in; she was carrying a basket piled high with fruit. She'd been officially discharged from the hospital, and now she was the one visiting a friend there.

"Thanks, you three," I told them. Natsunagi was going to school, Saikawa was working as an idol, and Charlie had various jobs to do. Whenever they had time, though, they came to visit Siesta.

"Um...?" However, Saikawa tilted her head curiously. For some reason, all three of them seemed either bewildered or put off.

"Why are you thanking us just for coming to visit Ma'am, Kimizuka? Exactly what are you to her, huh?" Charlie gave me a clammy look.

"You haven't been to school at all, Kimizuka. You're aaalways here with Siesta," Natsunagi said.

Saikawa and the others pointed at me, complaining.

Yeesh. What were they mad about? "Taking care of my partner is part of my job, isn't it?" As I said it, I was looking at Siesta.

She'd been asleep for the past week. So far, there hadn't been any drastic changes, and the seed's growth seemed to be suppressed. Someday we'd destroy that seed without harming the rest of her, or find some other way to wake her up safely. That was my wish and the goal of our current story.

"Your partner, hm?" The next thing I knew, Natsunagi was looking at my face.

"What?"

"Ohhh, nothing."

Geez. Not fair.

".......Heh-heh." I hadn't said it aloud, but she'd probably guessed what I was thinking. Smiling, she gazed at me for a long time. Then, finally, she tucked her short hair behind her ears and looked away.

This had been our daily routine ever since Siesta fell asleep. That day, something had decisively changed. However, there were other things that hadn't. I probably had one foot in this new routine, which wasn't like tepid water at all.

"Still, we're pretty short on time. We'll need to leave soon." Charlie checked her watch.

After this, we were headed out on a journey to a certain destination.

"All four of us, traveling together! I can't wait!" Saikawa twirled in place, giddy with the idea of our impending three-day trip.

"We're not going for fun, you know..."

We were responding to a summons from the Federation Government. They were holding an advisory council regarding Natsunagi's decision to inherit the position of Ace Detective, and the rest of us were going with her, timing our trip for the long September holiday. The venue for this one was in Singapore.

"I wonder if I'll get the chance to wear my new swimsuit..."

"You're the central figure here, but you're having the most fun with it." Natsunagi was giving me serious déjà vu.

"You want to see my swimsuit too, right, Kimizuka?"

I hadn't gotten to see it on the cruise ship, after all.

...In that case, yeah.

"Well, I guess we could get away with blowing one day on fun stuff." When I said that, a smile like summer sunshine lit up her face.

"All right, shall we go?" Saikawa stretched her arms toward the ceiling. "We'll be back, Siesta!" Waving energetically, she left the hospital room. And then...

"Ma'am, I'll come again as soon as we get home, I promise! What kind of souvenir would you like? Meat? Okay, I'll buy you lots of meat!"

Charlie spoke to Siesta in the same tone she always used...but then, with a smile that was just a little sad, she kissed Siesta's right hand, then left the room.

"In the end, I'm the only one who barely got to see her," Natsunagi murmured, gazing at Siesta's face. "There was so much I wanted to tell her and fight with her over..." The only time Natsunagi had gotten to meet Siesta was on that final battlefield. Having two ace detectives in the world at the same time was apparently even tougher than I'd imagined.

"Still, we'll meet again someday." Natsunagi pressed her lips together with determination.

Siesta and Natsunagi had met six years ago, and then again last year. I hoped from the bottom of my heart that I'd get to see the two of them reunite one day.

"I'll... No, we'll find a way to wake you up, I swear. Wait for us. Until then, you can leave the Ace Detective's will to me," she promised Siesta. Then, with a glance at me, she left the room.

"Singapore, huh? We went there together, way back when."

I recalled those distant memories. We'd played on the beach and played in the casinos...but as usual, we'd gotten pulled into crazy incidents, too. It was the same old trouble-ridden adventure tale. It was sort of nostalgic and, at the same time, something I never wanted to do again.

"...Still. One of these days, one more time..." We'd go somewhere, just the two of us. I remembered making that promise in New York while we watched the musical.

"Okay, I'll be back." I was the last one in the room. Gazing at Siesta's peaceful face, I told her, "I guess it'll be four days before we see each other again." I was a little reluctant to leave her.

There was no answer. Of course there wasn't.

The detective was already—

—No, she wasn't.

That's right. There's really no need to feel sad or uneasy.

After all, the detective's not dead anymore.

She's just settled down for a long, long nap.

# HAVE YOU BEEN TURNED ON TO LIGHT NOVELS YET?

## 86—EIGHTY-SIX, VOL. I–II

In truth, there is no such thing as a bloodless war. Beyond the fortified walls protecting the eighty-five Republic Sectors lies the "nonexistent" Eighty-Sixth Sector. The young men and women of this forsaken land are branded the Eighty-Six and, stripped of their humanity, pilot "unmanned" weapons into battle...

**Manga adaptation available now!**

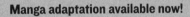